序 言

　　「篇章結構」是「指定科目考試」必考的題型，而且固定都佔十分。此外，在各校的月期考、複習考和模考中，也很常出現。所以不管你的目標是指考、推甄，還是申請入學，熟悉這種題型，都是非常重要的。

　　「篇章結構」這個大題，除了測驗英文程度之外，還考驗你的邏輯思考能力。通常整篇文章的長度都蠻長的，對於實力很強的考生來說，只要小心就可以拿到全部的分數，但是如果你沒有十足的把握，那麼平時就要多練習做題目，畢竟英文程度和邏輯觀念，都是可以靠訓練來增強的。

　　開始作答篇章結構這個大題時，要注意開頭的第一句話，因為那通常都是主題句，能夠引導你看懂整篇文章，即使文章很長也不必緊張，文章愈長，愈容易看出邏輯觀念。看到看不懂的字不用怕，因為不會考單字的意思，你只要看懂前後文，就可以找到正確的答案。在作答的時候，最好養成習慣把用過的選項作個記號，以免浪費時間重複考慮，或是不慎重複使用選項，白白丟掉分數。

　　在看文章內容時，速度要快，只要理解大意就可以，但是看選項的時候，就要仔細，要依照文意來選出最合理的句子。要特別注意空格前後的句子，因為**在前後文所出現的代名詞，如：this, them, these 等，通常會跟空格的主詞或受詞有關，是作答的關鍵。**如果有某個空格不確定要選哪個選項，不妨先跳過去，因為最後剩下來的選項，總會剛好符合那個空格。

　　本書雖經審慎編校，疏漏之處恐所難免，誠盼各界先進不吝批評指正。

編者　謹識

TEST 1

說明: 第1至5題,每題一個空格。請依文意在文章後所提供的(A)到
(E) 選項中分別選出最適當者。

___1___. Multi-story wonders topped with flashing
lights to beckon the birds home from training flights, the
coops can make the human habitations below them seem
cramped by comparison. ___2___. ___3___. Authorities
estimate there are around 600 pigeon racers around
Taipei's domestic airport alone. Each of them has a
flock of 200-300 birds. A few years ago, one of Taiwan's
prized Mirage fighter jets was grounded for more than one
million USD in repairs after a collision with a feathered
projectile. ___4___. As a result, there is now a 5 km
pigeon exclusion zone around Taiwan's airports. ___5___.

(A) Collisions between pigeons and planes are
    occurring at the rate of one a month
(B) Something had to give —— and it wasn't the jets
(C) Taipei's rooftop pigeon aviaries are the envy
    of the pigeon-racing world
(D) Those whose birds transgress will receive
    whopping fines
(E) But the birds can be bad news for humans who
    take to the sky

TEST 1 詳解

[1](C) Taipei's rooftop pigeon aviaries are the envy of the pigeon-racing world. Multi-story wonders topped with flashing lights to beckon the birds home from training flights, the coops can make the human habitations below them seem cramped by comparison.

整個賽鴿界都很羨慕台北屋頂的鴿籠。鴿籠分成好幾層，頂樓再加蓋閃爍的燈光，用來召喚鴿子們從訓練飛行中歸來，相較之下，人類在下面的住宅，似乎有點狹窄擁擠。

> rooftop (ˈrufˌtɑp) *n.* 屋頂　　pigeon (ˈpɪdʒən) *n.* 鴿子
> aviary (ˈeviˌɛrɪ) *n.* 鳥舍；鴿籠
> envy (ˈɛnvɪ) *n.* 羨慕的對象　　race (res) *v.* 比賽
> multi-story (ˌmʌltɪˈstɔrɪ) *adj.* 多層的
> wonder (ˈwʌndə) *n.* 神奇之物 (在此指鴿籠)
> **be topped with** 頂樓加蓋　　flashing (ˈflæʃɪŋ) *adj.* 閃爍的
> beckon (ˈbɛkən) *v.* 召喚　　coop (kup) *n.* 籠子
> habitation (ˌhæbəˈteʃən) *n.* 住宅
> cramped (kræmpt) *adj.* 狹窄的　　**by comparison** 相較之下

[2](E) But the birds can be bad news for humans who take to the sky.
[3](A) Collisions between pigeons and planes are occurring at the rate of one a month.

但是這些鴿子對於飛在空中的人，可能是個壞消息。鴿子和飛機相撞的事件，平均每個月發生一次。

> **take to the sky** 飛在空中　　collision (kəˈlɪʒən) *n.* 相撞
> **at the rate of** 以～比率

Authorities estimate there are around 600 pigeon racers around Taipei's domestic airport alone. Each of them has a flock of 200-300 birds. A few years ago, one of Taiwan's prized Mirage fighter jets was grounded for more than one million USD in repairs after a collision with a feathered projectile.

當局估計，單單在台北的國內機場（即松山機場）周邊，就有大約六百名賽鴿人士。他們每人養了二百到三百隻鴿子。幾年前，台灣一架珍貴的幻象戰鬥機，就是在與飛鳥撞擊後遭到停飛，維修費用超過一百萬美金。

> authorities〔ə'θɔrətɪz〕*n. pl.* 當局
> estimate〔'ɛstə,met〕*v.* 估計　　domestic〔də'mɛstɪk〕*adj.* 國內的
> alone〔ə'lon〕*adv.* 單單；僅僅
> flock〔flɑk〕*n.* （鳥）群　　prized〔praɪzd〕*adj.* 珍貴的
> mirage〔mə'rɑʒ〕*n.* 海市蜃樓；幻想
> ***Mirage fighter jet*** 幻象戰鬥機
> ground〔graʊnd〕*v.* （飛機）停飛
> feathered〔'fɛðəd〕*adj.* 有羽毛的
> projectile〔prə'dʒɛktḷ〕*n.* 發射物　　***feathered projectile*** 鳥

[4](B) Something had to give — and it wasn't the jets. As a result, there is now a 5 km pigeon exclusion zone around Taiwan's airports. [5](D) Those whose birds transgress will receive whopping fines.

某一邊必須讓步——而不會是飛機。因此，現在台灣的機場周邊，有五公里的鴿子禁區。只要鳥兒踰越禁區，飼主都將被處以巨額罰金。

> give〔gɪv〕*v.* 讓步；妥協　　***as a result*** 結果；因此
> exclusion〔ɪk'skluʒən〕*n.* 除外　　***exclusion zone*** 禁區
> transgress〔træns'grɛs〕*v.* 踰越
> whopping〔'hwɑpɪŋ〕*adj.* 極大的

TEST 2

說明： 第 1 至 5 題，每題一個空格。請依文意在文章後所提供的 (A) 到 (E) 選項中分別選出最適當者。

The black-faced spoonbill is one of the many species of migratory birds ___1___. It is also a bird that is on the verge of extinction. A news report noted recently that ___2___. However, according to a recent survey conducted by the Wild Bird Federation Taiwan, ___3___, mostly flying into Chiku, Tainan County. The black-faced spoonbill can be distinguished by its white body and more specifically by its black spoon-like beak, and ___4___. In Taiwan, the bird has been spotted at the mouth of the Lanyang River in Ilan County, the Tamsui River in Taipei County, at the mouth of the Tatun River in Changhua County, and also at the mouth of the Cheng-wen River in Tainan County. To protect the black-faced spoonbill ___5___ where Vice President Annette Lu was in attendance to show the government's determination to protect this very rare wild bird. The fair also attracted a number of domestic and foreign wildlife conservation groups, from Japan, Vietnam, South Korea, North Korea, and Hong Kong.

(A) it usually prefers to stay in shallow water areas where it can search for food

(B) there are less than 1,000 black-faced spoonbills left in the world

(C) a conservation fair was held at Chiku

(D) a total of 450 black-faced spoonbills had arrived in Taiwan this year

(E) which fly south to Taiwan from northern mainland China every year to spend the winter

TEST 2 詳解

The black-faced spoonbill is one of the many species of migratory birds [1](E) which fly south to Taiwan from northern mainland China every year to spend the winter. It is also a bird that is on the verge of extinction. A news report noted recently that [2](B) there are less than 1,000 black-faced spoonbills left in the world. However, according to a recent survey conducted by the Wild Bird Federation Taiwan, [3](D) a total of 450 black-faced spoonbills had arrived in Taiwan this year, mostly flying into Chiku, Tainan County.

每年有許多候鳥會從中國大陸北方，南飛到台灣來過冬，黑面琵鷺是其中之一。而牠也是瀕臨絕種的鳥類之一。最近一則新聞報導提到，全世界只剩下不到一千隻黑面琵鷺。然而，根據台灣的野鳥協會，最近所進行的一項調查指出，今年已到達台灣的黑面琵鷺，總數有四百五十隻，大多數都飛到台南縣的七股。

> bill (bɪl) *n.* 鳥嘴　　***black-faced spoonbill*** 黑面琵鷺
> species ('spiʃɪz) *n. pl.* 種 (單複數同形)
> migratory ('maɪgrə,torɪ) *adj.* 遷移的
> ***migratory bird*** 候鳥　　***on the verge of*** 瀕臨
> extinction (ɪk'stɪŋkʃən) *n.* 絕種　　note (not) *v.* 注意到；提出
> survey ('sɜve) *n.* 調查　　conduct (kən'dʌkt) *v.* 進行
> federation (,fɛdə'reʃən) *n.* 聯盟　　total ('totl̩) *n.* 總數

The black-faced spoonbill can be distinguished by its white body and more specifically by its black spoon-like beak, and [4](A) it usually prefers to stay in shallow water areas where it can search for food. In Taiwan, the bird has been spotted at the mouth of the Lanyang River in Ilan County, the Tamsui River in Taipei County, at the mouth of the Tatun River in Changhua County, and also at the mouth of the Cheng-wen River in Tainan County.

要區分黑面琵鷺，可以看牠全白的身體，特別是牠像湯匙般的黑色鳥嘴，牠通常比較喜歡待在淺水處，好尋找食物。在台灣，曾經發現黑面琵鷺的地區包括，宜蘭縣的蘭陽溪、台北縣的淡水河、彰化縣的大屯溪，及台南縣的曾文溪等河流的河口。

      distinguish (dɪ'stɪŋgwɪʃ) v. 區分
      specifically (spɪ'sɪfɪklɪ) adv. 特別地
      beak (bik) n. 鳥嘴　　shallow ('ʃælo) adj. 淺的
      spot (spɑt) v. 看到；發現　　mouth (mauθ) n. 河口；出海口

To protect the black-faced spoonbill [5](C) a conservation fair was held at Chiku where Vice President Annette Lu was in attendance to show the government's determination to protect this very rare wild bird. The fair also attracted a number of domestic and foreign wildlife conservation groups, from Japan, Vietnam, South Korea, North Korea, and Hong Kong.

為了保護黑面琵鷺，在七股舉辦了一場保育博覽會，副總統呂秀蓮女士也出席會場，以表示政府要保護這種稀有野鳥的決心。這場博覽會也吸引了許多，來自國內外的野生動物保育團體，包括日本、越南、南韓、北韓以及香港。

      conservation (ˌkɑnsə'veʃən) n. 保育　　fair (fɛr) n. 博覽會
      vice-president ('vaɪs'prɛzədənt) n. 副總統
      attendance (ə'tɛndəns) n. 出席
      determination (dɪˌtɝmə'neʃən) n. 決心
      rare (rɛr) adj. 稀有的　　wildlife ('waɪldˌlaɪf) n. 野生動物

TEST 3

說明： 第 1 至 5 題，每題一個空格。請依文意在文章後所提供的 (A) 到 (E) 選項中分別選出最適當者。

____1____ Scientists and experts have proved the uniqueness of fingerprints and discovered that no exactly identical pattern is passed on from parents to children, though nobody knows why this is the case.

The ridge structure on a person's fingers does not change with growth and is not affected by superficial injuries. Burns, cuts and other damage to the outer part of the skin will be replaced in time by new skin which bears a reproduction of the original pattern. ____2____ Some criminals make use of this fact to remove their own fingerprints, but this is a dangerous and rare step to take.

Fingerprints can be made very easily with printer's ink. They can be recorded easily. ____3____ Because of the simplicity and economy of this system, fingerprints have often been used as a

method of solving a criminal case. ___4___ His
fingerprints can prove who he is even if his
appearance has been changed by age or accident.

When a suspect leaves fingerprints behind at
the scene of a crime, they are difficult to detect with
the naked eye. ___5___ Some of the marks found
are incomplete but identification is possible if a
print a quarter of an inch square can be obtained.

(A) Special techniques are used to "develop"
them.
(B) A suspected man may deny a charge but
this may be in vain.
(C) With special methods, identification can
be achieved successfully within a short
time.
(D) Every human being has a unique
arrangement of skin on his fingers and
this arrangement is   unchangeable.
(E) It is only when the inner skin is injured
that the arrangement will be destroyed.

TEST 3 詳解

[1](**D**) Every human being has a unique arrangement of skin on his fingers and this arrangement is unchangeable. Scientists and experts have proved the uniqueness of fingerprints and discovered that no exactly identical pattern is passed on from parents to children, though nobody knows why this is the case.

每個人手指上的皮膚都有獨特的紋路，而這些紋路是無法改變的。科學家和專家已經證實，指紋是獨一無二的，並且也發現，父母無法將完全相同的指紋，遺傳給他們的子女，雖然沒有人知道，情況為何會如此。

> ***human being*** 人　　unique〔ju'nik〕*adj.* 獨特的；獨一無二的
> arrangement〔ə'rendʒmənt〕*n.* 排列方式；紋路
> unchangeable〔ʌn'tʃendʒəbḷ〕*adj.* 無法改變的
> expert〔'ɛkspɜt〕*n.* 專家　　prove〔pruv〕*v.* 證實
> uniqueness〔ju'niknɪs〕*n.* 獨特性
> fingerprint〔'fɪŋgɚˌprɪnt〕*n.* 指紋
> identical〔aɪ'dɛntɪkḷ〕*adj.* 完全相同的
> pattern〔'pætən〕*n.* 圖案
> ***pass on*** 傳給　　***the case*** 事實；真相

The ridge structure on a person's fingers does not change with growth and is not affected by superficial injuries. Burns, cuts and other damage to the outer part of the skin will be replaced in time by new skin which bears a reproduction of the original pattern.

一個人手指上的指紋，並不會隨著成長而改變，也不會因為表皮受到傷害而受影響。燒傷、割傷，和其他傷及表皮的傷口，遲早都會被新的皮膚所取代，而這些皮膚則會具有和原來一模一樣的指紋。

ridge〔rɪdʒ〕*n.* 稜紋

structure〔'strʌktʃə〕*n.* 結構　　***ridge structure*** 指紋

growth〔groθ〕*n.* 生長　　superficial〔ˌsupə'fɪʃəl〕*adj.* 表皮的

injury〔'ɪndʒərɪ〕*n.* 傷害　　burn〔bɜn〕*n.* 燒傷

cut〔kʌt〕*n.* 割傷　　replace〔rɪ'ples〕*v.* 取代

in time 遲早；最終　　bear〔bɛr〕*v.* 具有

reproduction〔ˌriprə'dʌkʃən〕*n.* 複製

original〔ə'rɪdʒənḷ〕*adj.* 原來的

pattern〔'pætən〕*n.* 紋路；圖案

²**(E)** It is only when the inner skin is injured that the arrangement will be destroyed.　Some criminals make use of this fact to remove their own fingerprints, but this is a dangerous and rare step to take. 只有當內層皮膚受到傷害，紋路才會被破壞。有些罪犯會利用這個原理，除去其本身的指紋，但採取這個步驟，是非常危險而且罕見的。

inner〔'ɪnə〕*adj.* 內層的　　destroy〔dɪ'strɔɪ〕*v.* 破壞

criminal〔'krɪmənḷ〕*n.* 罪犯　　***make use of*** 利用

fact〔fækt〕*n.* 事實；論據　　remove〔rɪ'muv〕*v.* 除去

rare〔rɛr〕*adj.* 罕見的　　take〔tek〕*v.* 採取

Fingerprints can be made very easily with printer's ink.　They can be recorded easily.　³**(C)** With special methods, identification can be achieved successfully within a short time.　Because of the simplicity and economy of this system, fingerprints have often been used as a method of solving a criminal case.　⁴**(B)** A suspected man may deny a charge but this may be in vain.　His fingerprints can prove who he is even if his appearance has been changed by age or accident.

用印刷油墨，可以非常輕易地印出指紋。指紋很容易就可以被記錄下來。利用特殊的方法，就可以在短時間內成功地辨識指紋。因為這種方法既簡單又省錢，所以指紋經常被用來作為偵破刑事案件的方法。嫌疑犯可能會否認某項指控，但這樣做可能會徒勞無功，因為指紋可以證明其身分，即使他的外表已隨著年紀增長，或因為意外，而有所改變。

> ***printer's ink*** 印刷油墨　　**record** (rɪˋkɔrd) *v.* 記錄
> **identification** (aɪ,dɛntəfəˋkeʃən) *n.* 辨識；確認
> **achieve** (əˋtʃiv) *v.* 做到　　**simplicity** (,sɪmˋplɪsətɪ) *n.* 簡單
> **economy** (ɪˋkɑnəmɪ) *n.* 省錢
> **system** (ˋsɪstəm) *n.* 方法　　***criminal case*** 刑事案件
> **suspected** (səˋspɛktɪd) *adj.* 有嫌疑的　　**deny** (dɪˋnaɪ) *v.* 否認
> **charge** (tʃɑrdʒ) *n.* 指控　　***in vain*** 徒勞無功
> ***even if*** 即使　　**appearance** (əˋpɪrəns) *n.* 外表

When a suspect leaves fingerprints behind at the scene of a crime, they are difficult to detect with the naked eye. [5](A) Special techniques are used to "develop" them. Some of the marks found are incomplete but identification is possible if a print a quarter of an inch square can   obtained.

當嫌疑犯將指紋遺留在犯罪現場時，那是很難用肉眼看出來的。可以使用特殊的技巧，使它們「顯現出來」。有些被發現的痕跡是不完整的，但如果能獲得四分之一英吋見方的指紋，還是有可能完成辨識的工作。

> **suspect** (ˋsʌspɛkt) *n.* 嫌疑犯　　***leave ~ behind*** 遺留
> **scene** (sin) *n.* 現場　　**detect** (dɪˋtɛkt) *v.* 查出；發現
> ***the naked eye*** 肉眼　　**technique** (tɛkˋnik) *n.* 技巧
> **develop** (dɪˋvɛləp) *v.* 使顯像　　**mark** (mɑrk) *n.* 痕跡
> **incomplete** (,ɪnkəmˋplit) *adj.* 不完整的
> **print** (prɪnt) *n.* 指紋 (= *fingerprint*)
> ***a quarter of an inch square*** 1/4 英吋見方【= 1/4 × 1/4 = 1/16 (平方英吋)】

TEST 4

說明： 第 1 至 5 題，每題一個空格。請依文意在文章後所提供的 (A) 到
(E) 選項中分別選出最適當者。

____1____ You usually feel happier on sunny days than
you do on cloudy days. For most people, these minor
differences in mood are not serious. ____2____

People suffering from SAD are much more sensitive to
the mood altering effects of sunlight. ____3____ Teenagers
with SAD may shout at their parents, argue with their
friends, or have major difficulty with schoolwork.

____4____ Our bodies are regulated by a natural clock,
which is set by the light/dark cycles of sunlight. ____5____
This leads to the production of a hormone, melatonin, at the
wrong time of the day. Melatonin is associated with anger.

(A) As the winter approaches and there is less daylight,
they become depressed.
(B) People who develop SAD appear to have a
disturbance in their body's clock.
(C) Sunshine affects your mood.
(D) However, nearly two million people in the U.S.
suffer from "seasonal affective disorder," or SAD.
(E) Why does this happen?

TEST 4 詳解

[1](C) Sunshine affects your mood. You usually feel happier on sunny days than you do on cloudy days. For most people, these minor differences in mood are not serious.

陽光會影響你的情緒。通常在晴天，你的心情會比陰天好。對大多數人來說，這些情緒上的變化並不嚴重。

> affect〔əˈfɛkt〕*v.* 影響　　mood〔mud〕*n.* 情緒
> minor〔ˈmaɪnə〕*adj.* 輕微的

[2](D) However, nearly two million people in the U.S. suffer from "seasonal affective disorder," or SAD.

然而在美國，卻有將近兩百萬的人，罹患「季節性情緒失調」，或稱SAD。

> ***suffer from*** 罹患（病、痛）
> seasonal〔ˈsiznəl〕*adj.* 季節性的
> affective〔əˈfɛktɪv〕*adj.* 情緒上的
> disorder〔dɪsˈɔrdə〕*n.* 失調
> ***seasonal affective disorder*** 季節性情緒失調

People suffering from SAD are much more sensitive to the mood altering effects of sunlight. [3](A) As the winter approaches and there is less daylight, they become depressed. Teenagers with SAD may shout at their parents, argue with their friends, or have major difficulty with schoolwork.

　　罹患 SAD 的人，對於陽光引起的情緒變化，比一般人敏感多了。
隨著冬天來臨，白晝變短，他們就會變得很沮喪。罹患 SAD 的青少年，
可能會對父母吼叫，和朋友吵架，並在學習上有較多障礙。

sensitive ('sɛnsətɪv) *adj.* 敏感的　　altering ('ɔltərɪŋ) *adj.* 改變的
approach (ə'protʃ) *v.* 接近　　daylight ('de,laɪt) *n.* 日光
depressed (dɪ'prɛst) *adj.* 沮喪的
major ('medʒɚ) *adj.* 較多的

[4](E) Why does this happen?　Our bodies are regulated by a
natural clock, which is set by the light/dark cycles of sunlight.

　　爲什麼會產生這種症狀呢？我們的身體都是由生理時鐘所控制，而
這個生理時鐘，是由晝夜輪替所設定。

regulate ('rɛgjə,let) *v.* 調節；控制　　set (sɛt) *v.* 設定
cycle ('saɪkl̩) *n.* 循環

[5](B) People who develop SAD appear to have a disturbance in
their body's clock.　This leads to the production of a hormone,
melatonin, at the wrong time of the day.　Melatonin is associated with
anger.

　　SAD 患者似乎是生理時鐘的運作不協調。這會導致身體在錯誤的時
段，分泌褪黑激素這種荷爾蒙。褪黑激素和發脾氣有關。

develop (dɪ'vɛləp) *v.* 罹患（病）
appear to + *V.* 似乎　　disturbance (dɪ'stɝbəns) *n.* 擾亂
lead to 導致　　production (prə'dʌkʃən) *n.* 生產
hormone ('hɔrmon) *n.* 荷爾蒙
melatonin (,mɛlə'tonɪn) *n.* 褪黑激素
be associated with 和～有關　　anger ('æŋgɚ) *n.* 發怒

TEST 5

說明： 第 1 至 5 題，每題一個空格。請依文意在文章後所提供的 (A) 到 (E) 選項中分別選出最適當者。

Thomas van Beek, a Dutch businessman, was starting out in business. He needed an efficient secretary to help him. Van Beek interviewed many people, but none seemed good enough for the job.

Finally, van Beek interviewed Ms. Neef. ___1___ Besides her fine office skills, Ms. Neef had a gracious personality. Van Beek decided to hire her.

After only one week, van Beek was convinced he had made the right choice. Ms. Neef ran the office smoothly. She handled all calls politely. She managed to stay unruffled, even when an emergency came up. Ms. Neef was also tireless. ___2___

For 12 years Ms. Neef continued to do her job excellently. She seemed to be able to do the work of two people. ___3___ Van Beek reluctantly accepted her decision.

Van Beek organized a good-bye party to show his appreciation to Ms. Neef. ___4___ Two Ms. Neefs showed up at the party. They were identical twins. The sisters had shared the job as van Beek's secretary. ___5___ For 12 years, van Beek never suspected that he had really hired two secretaries instead of one.

(A) Even when her boss ran out of energy, Ms. Neef displayed an unlimited amount of pep.

(B) At the party, the boss learned the secret of how his faithful secretary had managed to have so much energy.

(C) Each worked half-time and split the paycheck.

(D) Her typing and shorthand skills were exceptional.

(E) Then, Ms. Neef announced that she planned to retire.

TEST 5 詳解

Thomas van Beek, a Dutch businessman, was starting out in business. He needed an efficient secretary to help him. Van Beek interviewed many people, but none seemed good enough for the job.

湯瑪士范畢克是荷蘭商人，他想要開始做生意。他需要一位手腳快的秘書來幫他。來和范畢克先生面談的人很多，可是似乎沒有人可以勝任這份工作。

> Dutch〔dʌtʃ〕*adj.* 荷蘭的　　　***start out*** 開始
> efficient〔ə'fɪʃənt〕*adj.* 有效率的
> secretary〔'sɛkrə,tɛrɪ〕*n.* 秘書　　　seem〔sim〕*v.* 似乎
> interview〔'ɪntə,vju〕*v.* 與～面談

Finally, van Beek interviewed Ms. Neef. [1](D) Her typing and shorthand skills were exceptional. Besides her fine office skills, Ms. Neef had a gracious personality. Van Beek decided to hire her.

後來，有一位妮芙女士來和范畢克先生面試。她打字和速記的能力一流。除了絕佳的辦公能力外，妮芙女士個性非常親切。范畢克馬上決定僱用她。

> finally〔'faɪnl̩ɪ〕*adv.* 最後　　　typing〔'taɪpɪŋ〕*n.* 打字
> shorthand〔'ʃɔrt,hænd〕*n.* 速記
> skill〔skɪl〕*n.* 技術；技巧
> exceptional〔ɪk'sɛpʃənl̩〕*adj.* 優秀的
> besides〔bɪ'saɪdz〕*prep.* 除…之外
> gracious〔'greʃəs〕*adj.* 親切的
> personality〔,pɜsn̩'ælətɪ〕*n.* 個性
> decide〔dɪ'saɪd〕*v.* 決定　　　hire〔haɪr〕*v.* 僱用

After only one week, van Beek was convinced he had made the right choice. Ms. Neef ran the office smoothly. She handled all calls politely.

才過了一個禮拜，范畢克就確信他的選擇是對的。妮芙女士把辦公室管理得有條不紊，所有的來電都能對答合宜。

> convince (kən'vɪns) v. 使確信
> choice (tʃɔɪs) n. 選擇　　run (rʌn) v. 管理
> smoothly ('smuðlɪ) adv. 順利地
> handle ('hændḷ) v. 處理　　politely (pə'laɪtlɪ) adv. 有禮地

She managed to stay unruffled, even when an emergency came up. Ms. Neef was also tireless. **²(A) Even when her boss ran out of energy, Ms. Neef displayed an unlimited amount of pep.**

就算是有緊急事故發生，她也能設法保持鎮定。還有，妮芙女士從來都不喊累。即使連她老闆都累了，妮芙女士仍然展現了用不完的精力。

> ***manage to + V.*** 設法
> unruffled (ʌn'rʌfḷd) adj. 平靜的
> emergency (ɪ'mɝdʒənsɪ) n. 緊急　　***come up*** 發生
> tireless ('taɪrlɪs) adj. 不會疲倦的　　***run out of*** 用完
> energy ('ɛnədʒɪ) n. 精力　　display (dɪ'sple) v. 使展現
> unlimited (ʌn'lɪmɪtɪd) adj. 無限的　　pep (pɛp) n. 精力

For 12 years Ms. Neef continued to do her job excellently. She seemed to be able to do the work of two people. **³(E) Then, Ms. Neef announced that she planned to retire.** Van Beek reluctantly accepted her decision.

十二年來，妮芙女士在工作上一直表現得很出色。她似乎能夠做兩人
份的工作。後來，妮芙女士宣佈她想退休了。范畢克先生很不情願地接受
她的決定。

> announce〔ə'naʊns〕v. 宣佈　　retire〔rɪ'taɪr〕v. 退休
> reluctantly〔rɪ'lʌktəntlɪ〕adv. 不情願地

Van Beek organized a good-bye party to show his appreciation
to Ms. Neef. <u>⁴(B) At the party, the boss learned the secret of how his
faithful secretary had managed to have so much energy.</u> Two Ms.
Neefs showed up at the party.

　　為了表達他對妮芙女士的感激之意，范畢克先生替她辦了一個惜別
會。在惜別會上，這個老闆終於知道，為什麼這位忠實的秘書，總是精
力旺盛的祕密。有兩位妮芙女士出現在惜別會上。

> organize〔'ɔrgən,aɪz〕v. 舉辦
> appreciation〔ə,priʃɪ'eʃən〕n. 感激
> faithful〔'feθfəl〕adj. 忠實的　　***show up*** 出現

They were identical twins. The sisters had shared the job as van
Beek's secretary. <u>⁵(C) Each worked half-time and split the paycheck.</u>
For 12 years, van Beek never suspected that he had really hired two
secretaries instead of one.

　　原來她們是雙胞胎。這對姊妹花一起分擔范畢克的秘書這份工作。她
們每個人只做半天，並把薪水對分。這十二年來，范畢克先生從來都沒有
懷疑過，原來他僱用了兩個秘書，而不是一個。

> identical〔aɪ'dɛntɪkl̩〕adj. 相同的
> ***identical twin*** 同卵雙胞胎　　split〔splɪt〕v. 分開
> paycheck〔'pe,tʃɛk〕n. 付薪水的支票；薪水
> ***instead of*** 而不是

TEST 6

說明： 第 1 至 5 題，每題一個空格。請依文意在文章後所提供的(A)到
(E) 選項中分別選出最適當者。

Japanese culture has succeeded in moving overseas in the past decade. ___1___ For example, Pokemon has been translated into several languages. Karaoke, pronounced 'carry oh key' in English, has now become a permanent part of popular culture in many cultures. ___2___ Japanese movies are also popular in foreign countries. ___3___ Japanese food is also experiencing a boom in foreign countries. There are plenty of sushi restaurants worldwide, as well as ramen shops. And you can buy Japanese beer almost everywhere. Even Japanese fashion designers, such as Kenzo, are enjoying great popularity in foreign countries. ___4___ You will never forget the Japanese football player Hide Nakata, who has become a hero even in Italy. ___5___

(A) The 2002 FIFA just came to an end a couple of months ago.

(B) Most British pubs have special nights each week when people can sing their favorite songs.

(C) Akira Kurosawa has won so many prizes in major film festivals.

(D) Young people in America, Asia and Europe watch a lot of Japanese cartoons and read Japanese comics.

(E) The trend will probably become even stronger in the future.

TEST 6　詳解

Japanese culture has succeeded in moving overseas in the past decade. [1](D) <u>Young people in America, Asia and Europe watch a lot of Japanese cartoons and read Japanese comics.</u> For example, Pokemon has been translated into several languages.

日本文化在過去十年已經成功地轉移到海外。美國、亞洲及歐洲的年輕人都看很多日本卡通和日本漫畫。舉例來說，口袋怪獸就已經被翻譯成好幾種語言。

Japanese〔,dʒæpə'niz〕*adj.* 日本的
culture〔'kʌltʃə〕*n.* 文化　　***succeed in*** 在～方面獲得成功
decade〔'dɛked〕*n.* 十年　　cartoon〔kɑr'tun〕*n.* 卡通
comic〔'kɑmɪk〕*n.* 漫畫　　translate〔træns'let〕*v.* 翻譯

Karaoke, pronounced 'carry oh key' in English, has now become a permanent part of popular culture in many cultures. [2](B) <u>Most British pubs have special nights each week when people can sing their favorite songs.</u> Japanese movies are also popular in foreign countries. [3](C) <u>Akira Kurosawa has won so many prizes in major film festivals.</u>

卡拉 OK，英文發音是 "carry oh key"，現在已變成許多文化當中，通俗文化永久不變的一環。大部分的英國酒吧，每個禮拜都有特別的幾個晚上，讓人們唱他們最喜歡的歌。日本電影在外國也大受歡迎。黑澤明在大型影展中也贏得許多獎項。

pronounce〔prə'nauns〕*v.* 發音
permanent〔'pɜmənənt〕*adj.* 永久的；不變的
prize〔praɪz〕*n.* 獎項　　***film festival*** 影展

Japanese food is also experiencing a boom in foreign countries. There are plenty of sushi restaurants worldwide, as well as ramen shops. And you can buy Japanese beer almost everywhere. Even Japanese fashion designers, such as Kenzo, are enjoying great popularity in foreign countries.

日本食物在國外也同樣十分興盛。世界各地都有很多壽司餐廳以及拉麵店。而且幾乎到處都可以買到日本啤酒。甚至日本的時裝設計師,如高田賢三,在外國也一樣大受歡迎。

> experience (ɪk'spɪrɪəns) *v.* 經歷
> boom (bum) *n.* 興盛　　sushi ('susɪ) *n.* 壽司
> worldwide ('wɜld'waɪd) *adv.* 在全世界
> ***as well as*** 以及　　***ramen*** 拉麵
> beer (bɪr) *n.* 啤酒　　fashion ('fæʃən) *n.* 時裝
> designer (dɪ'zaɪnə) *n.* 設計師
> popularity (ˌpɑpjə'lærətɪ) *n.* 名氣;討人喜歡

[4](A) The 2002 FIFA just came to an end a couple of months ago. You will never forget the Japanese football player Hide Nakata, who has become a hero even in Italy. [5](E) The trend will probably become even stronger in the future.

2002 年的世界盃足球賽,幾個月前才剛剛結束。你永遠也不會忘記日本足球球員中田英壽,他即使在義大利,也是個英雄。這種趨勢在未來可能會越演越烈。

> ***FIFA*** 國際足球聯盟 (= *Federation Internationale de Football Association*)　***come to an end*** 結束;停止 (= *end*)
> hero ('hɪro) *n.* 英雄　　trend (trɛnd) *n.* 趨勢

TEST 7

說明： 第 1 至 5 題，每題一個空格。請依文意在文章後所提供的 (A) 到 (E) 選項中分別選出最適當者。

You start to introduce an old friend to someone, and suddenly you can't remember that someone's name — even though you sense it just beyond the grasp of your memory. ___1___ Such tip-of-the-tongue — or TOT — incidents happen to almost everyone, notes Debroah Burke, a psychologist at Pomona College, California.

___2___ "Often, the sound of a word is arbitrary and senseless," says Burke. This sheer arbitrariness sometimes can make word retrieval challenging.

___3___ "I tell clients to do what salespeople often do — repeat a person's name several times just before you plan to see him," says psychologist Liz Zelinski of the University of Southern California in Los Angeles.

___4___ Burke tells the story of a student who was trying to remember the name of a particular recreational vehicle. The student wanted the word Winnebago, but she could only come up with rutabaga. When this happens, shift your focus to something else, suggests Burke. ___5___

(A) A TOT experience can seem worse when a similar-sounding, but incorrect, word pops into your head and stays there.

(B) Or you can't quite retrieve the name of a movie you just saw.

(C) The best way to prevent the problem is to use the name of a person or object as frequently as possible.

(D) These lapses have nothing to do with remembering the meaning of a word, but rather with its sound.

(E) "If you stop fretting about it, the correct word eventually will come to you."

TEST 7 詳解

You start to introduce an old friend to someone, and suddenly you can't remember that someone's name — even though you sense it just beyond the grasp of your memory.

你開始要介紹一位老朋友給某人認識，而突然間你卻不記得那個某人的名字——即使你察覺自己剛剛才忘掉他的名字。

sense〔sɛns〕v. 察覺　　grasp〔græsp〕n. 抓住；理解力
memory〔'mɛmərɪ〕n. 記憶

[1](B) Or you can't quite retrieve the name of a movie you just saw. Such tip-of-the-tongue — or TOT — incidents happen to almost everyone, notes Debroah Burke, a psychologist at Pomona College, California.

或者你才剛看過一部電影，但卻想不太起來電影名稱。這種話到嘴邊卻說不出來的經驗——簡稱為 TOT 事件——幾乎在每個人身上都會發生，這是加州帕馬諾學院的心理學家，黛柏拉柏克所提到的。

retrieve〔rɪ'triv〕v. 取回；想起
tip-of-the-tongue 話到嘴邊卻說不出來（此複合名詞來自於片語
　on the tip of one's tongue 話到嘴邊卻說不出來）
incident〔'ɪnsədənt〕n. 事件　　note〔not〕v. 提到
psychologist〔saɪ'kɑlədʒɪst〕n. 心理學家

[2](D) These lapses have nothing to do with remembering the meaning of a word, but rather with its sound. "Often, the sound of a word is arbitrary and senseless," says Burke.

這些失誤與是否記得一個字的意義無關，而與該字的發音有關。
柏克說：「通常，一個字的發音是很隨意、且無意義的。」

lapse〔læps〕 *n.* 失誤　　***have nothing to do with*** 與～無關
rather〔'ræðɚ〕 *adv.* 相反地　　arbitrary〔'ɑrbə,trɛrɪ〕 *adj.* 隨意的
senseless〔'sɛnslɪs〕 *adj.* 無意義的

This sheer arbitrariness sometimes can make word retrieval
challenging. [3](C) The best way to prevent the problem is to use
the name of a person or object as frequently as possible.

光是單純的隨意發音，有時會使想起一個字，變得很有挑戰性。避免
這個問題最好的方法就是，儘可能經常使用一個人或物體的名字。

sheer〔ʃɪr〕 *adj.* 單純的
arbitrariness〔'ɑrbə,trɛrɪnɪs〕 *n.* 隨意
retrieval〔rɪ'trivl̩〕 *n.* 取回；想起
challenging〔'tʃælɪndʒɪŋ〕 *adj.* 有挑戰性的
frequently〔'frikwəntlɪ〕 *adv.* 經常地

"I tell clients to do what salespeople often do — repeat a person's
name several times just before you plan to see him," says
psychologist Liz Zelinski of the University of Southern
California in Los Angeles.

「我叫客戶要用業務員常常使用的方法——就在計劃去見某人之前，覆
誦對方的名字數次，」南加大洛杉磯分校的心理學家，莉茲季林斯基
說道。

client〔'klaɪənt〕 *n.* 客戶
salespeople〔'selz,pipl̩〕 *n. pl.* 業務員
repeat〔rɪ'pit〕 *v.* 重複地說　　client〔'klaɪənt〕 *n.* 客戶

[4](A) A TOT experience can seem worse when a similar-sounding, but incorrect, word pops into your head and stays there. Burke tells the story of a student who was trying to remember the name of a particular recreational vehicle.

如果有一個發音相似、但意義不正確的字，突然出現並停留在你的腦海中，那麼 TOT 經驗可能會更嚴重。柏克就提到一個學生的故事，她試著要想起某種休閒車的名字。

similar〔'sɪmələ〕*adj.* 相似的
sounding〔'saʊndɪŋ〕*adj.* 有…聲音的
incorrect〔,ɪnkə'rɛkt〕*adj.* 不正確的
pop into 突然進入　　recreational〔,rɛkrɪ'eʃənḷ〕*adj.* 休閒的
vehicle〔'viɪkḷ〕*n.* 車輛

The student wanted the word Winnebago, but she could only come up with rutabaga. When this happens, shift your focus to something else, suggests Burke. [5](E) "If you stop fretting about it, the correct word eventually will come to you."

她要說的字是 Winnebago，但她卻只能想到 rutabaga。柏克建議，當這種情形發生時，把你的焦點轉移到其他事情上。「只要你不再煩惱這件事，正確的字最後一定會出現。」

Winnebago〔,wɪnɪ'bego〕*n.* 一種大型休閒車的品牌名稱
rutabaga〔,rutə'begə〕*n.* 瑞典蕪菁（蔬菜名）
come up with 想出（主意、計劃等）
shift〔ʃɪft〕*v.* 轉移 *< to >*　　focus〔'fokəs〕*n.* 焦點；中心
fret〔frɛt〕*v.* 煩惱 *< about >*
eventually〔ɪ'vɛntʃʊəlɪ〕*adv.* 最後

TEST 8

說明: 第 1 至 5 題,每題一個空格。請依文意在文章後所提供的(A)到
(E) 選項中分別選出最適當者。

____1____ Probably since the first rains fell on the newly-
formed planet. ____2____ produce sulfur or nitrogen compounds.
Lightning bolts form NO_2 from the nitrogen in the earth's
atmosphere. ____3____, this atmospheric "pollution" can serve
as a wholesome, gentle way of fertilizing the landscape.

____4____, when man intruded with a cloud of coal smoke
that symbolized the start of the industrial revolution. Suddenly,
sulfur and nitrogen that had accumulated in fossil fuels for
millions of years were being released as rapidly as coal could
be burned. ____5____ Today, a large coal-fired power plant can
emit in a single year as much sulfur dioxide as was blown out
by the May 18, 1980 eruption of Mount St. Helens in
Washington state — some 400,000 tons.

(A) Swiftly the volume of man-made pollutants gained
on nature's.

(B) When administered in nature's measured doses

(C) How long have we had acid rain?

(D) Volcanic eruptions, forest fires, and even the slow
bacterial decomposition of organic matter

(E) But this natural cycle began to give way about two
centuries ago

TEST 8 詳解

[1](C) How long have we had acid rain? Probably since the first rains fell on the newly-formed planet. [2](D) Volcanic eruptions, forest fires, and even the slow bacterial decomposition of organic matter produce sulfur or nitrogen compounds. Lightning bolts form NO_2 from the nitrogen in the earth's atmosphere.

酸雨已經存在多久了？可能從地球剛形成時，所下的第一場雨就有酸雨了。火山爆發、森林大火，甚至有機物質緩慢的細菌分解作用，都會產生硫或氮的化合物。因為地球的大氣層中有氮氣，所以閃電會形成二氧化氮。

> acid ('æsɪd) adj. 酸性的　**acid rain** 酸雨
> newly-formed ('njulɪ'fɔrmd) adj. 新形成的
> planet ('plænɪt) n. 行星（在此指「地球」）
> volcanic (vɑl'kænɪk) adj. 火山的
> eruption (ɪ'rʌpʃən) n. 爆發　　forest ('fɔrɪst) n. 森林
> bacterial (bæk'tɪrɪəl) adj. 細菌的
> decomposition (ˌdikɑmpə'zɪʃən) n. 分解
> organic (ɔr'gænɪk) adj. 有機的　**organic matter** 有機物質
> sulfur ('sʌlfə) n. 硫　　nitrogen ('naɪtrədʒən) n. 氮
> compound ('kɑmpaʊnd) n. 化合物　**lightning bolt** 閃電
> atmosphere ('ætməsˌfɪr) n. 大氣層

[3](B) When administered in nature's measured doses, this atmospheric "pollution" can serve as a wholesome, gentle way of fertilizing the landscape. 當這種大氣「污染」被控制在自然界的標準量時，它就可以被當作一種有益，而且溫和的方式，來使地表變肥沃。

> administer (əd'mɪnɪstə) v. 掌管；管理
> measured ('mɛʒəd) adj. 按標準定的　dose (dos) n. 劑量；份量
> atmospheric (ˌætməs'fɛrɪk) adj. 大氣的
> **serve as** 充當；作為　wholesome ('holsəm) adj. 有益的
> gentle ('dʒɛntḷ) adj. 溫和的　fertilize ('fɜtḷˌaɪz) v. 使肥沃
> landscape ('lændˌskep) n. 地表；風景

⁴(**E**) <u>But this natural cycle began to give way about two centuries</u> <u>ago</u>, when man intruded with a cloud of coal smoke that symbolized the start of the industrial revolution.　Suddenly, sulfur and nitrogen that had accumulated in fossil fuels for millions of years were being released as rapidly as coal could be burned.

　　但是這種自然的循環，在大約二百年前，就開始崩潰了，當時人類用一股煤煙，干擾了大自然，而這股煙就象徵了工業革命的開始。突然間，數百萬年來積聚在石化燃料裡的硫和氮，都被釋放到空氣中，其速度和燃燒煤的速度一樣快。

cycle〔'saɪk!〕*n.* 循環　　***give way*** 讓步；失去控制；崩潰
intrude〔ɪn'trud〕*v.* 入侵；干擾　　***a cloud of smoke*** 一股煙
coal〔kol〕*n.* 煤　　symbolize〔'sɪmb!͵aɪz〕*v.* 象徵
industrial revolution 工業革命　　suddenly〔'sʌdn̩lɪ〕*adv.* 突然地
accumulate〔ə'kjumjə͵let〕*v.* 積聚；累積　　fossil〔'fɑs!〕*n.* 化石
fuel〔'fjuəl〕*n.* 燃料　　***fossil fuel*** 石化燃料（如煤、石油、天然氣等）
release〔rɪ'lis〕*v.* 釋放　　rapidly〔'ræpɪdlɪ〕*adv.* 快速地

⁵(**A**) <u>Swiftly the volume of man-made pollutants gained on nature's.</u> Today, a large coal-fired power plant can emit in a single year as much sulfur dioxide as was blown out by the May 18, 1980 eruption of Mount St. Helens in Washington state — some 400,000 tons.

　　很快地，人造污染物的量，就趕上了大自然的。現在一座大型火力發電廠，一年內排放出的二氧化硫的量，就跟 1980 年 5 月 18 日，在華盛頓州爆發的聖海倫斯火山噴出的量一樣多 —— 大約四十萬公噸。

swiftly〔'swɪftlɪ〕*adv.* 很快地　　volume〔'vɑljəm〕*n.* 量
man-made〔'mæn͵med〕*adj.* 人造的
pollutant〔pə'lutn̩t〕*n.* 污染物　　***gain on*** 逼近；趕上
coal-fired〔'kol͵faɪrd〕*adj.* 燒煤的；用煤作燃料的
power plant 發電廠　　emit〔ɪ'mɪt〕*v.* 排放
single〔'sɪŋg!〕*adj.* 單一的　　dioxide〔daɪ'ɑksaɪd〕*n.* 二氧化物
sulfur dioxide 二氧化硫　　***blow out*** 噴出
Mount〔maunt〕*n.* ～山；～峰　　state〔stet〕*n.* 州
some〔sʌm〕*adv.* 大約　　ton〔tʌn〕*n.* 公噸

TEST 9

說明： 第 1 至 5 題，每題一個空格。請依文意在文章後所提供的 (A) 到 (E) 選項中分別選出最適當者。

Today's trumpet is one of the world's oldest instruments. ___1___ Although it looks nothing like its ancestors, there are many similarities. ___2___ They are all blown. And they all use the player's lips to produce the basic sound.

___3___ They wanted to create an instrument that would produce a beautiful and attractive tone, enable the performer to play all the notes of the scale, extend the range higher and lower, make it possible to play more difficult music and, in general, be easier to play well. ___4___

The trumpet family is much more than a group of related instruments that can stir one with their sound. It is much more than narrow tubes that are capable of producing a wide variety of musical

sounds. ___5___ From the use of trumpets in
ancient religious ceremonies to the important
part they play in modern rock bands, the trumpet
family of instruments has much to tell us about
civilization and its development.

(A) All trumpets are hollow tubes.

(B) The trumpet developed as players and
makers worked to improve its design,
size, shape and material.

(C) It is a link to many different periods of
history and to people of many cultures.

(D) It is the result of many centuries of
development.

(E) The remarkable way in which the
modern trumpet achieves these goals
is a measure of the success of all those
who struggled to perfect this
instrument.

TEST 9 詳解

Today's trumpet is one of the world's oldest instruments. ¹**(D) It is the result of many centuries of development.** Although it looks nothing like its ancestors, there are many similarities. ²**(A) All trumpets are hollow tubes.** They are all blown. And they all use the player's lips to produce the basic sound. 今日的喇叭，是世界上最古老的樂器之一。這是經過好幾世紀發展的成果。雖然它看起來一點也不像早期的喇叭，但是卻有許多相似之處。所有的喇叭都是中空的管子。它們都是用吹的。而且它們都是用吹奏者的嘴唇，來製造基本的聲音。

> trumpet (ˈtrʌmpɪt) *n.* 喇叭　　instrument (ˈɪnstrəmənt) *n.* 樂器
> ancestor (ˈænsɛstə) *n.* 祖先　　similarity (ˌsɪməˈlærətɪ) *n.* 類似
> hollow (ˈhɑlo) *adj.* 中空的　　tube (tjub) *n.* 管子　　blow (blo) *v.* 吹
> lips (lɪps) *n. pl.* 嘴唇　　produce (prəˈdjus) *v.* 產生

³**(B) The trumpet developed as players and makers worked to improve its design, size, shape and material.** They wanted to create an instrument that would produce a beautiful and attractive tone, enable the performer to play all the notes of the scale, extend the range higher and lower, make it possible to play more difficult music and, in general, be easier to play well.

喇叭之所以會進化，是由於吹奏者以及製造者，努力改進它的設計、大小、形狀和材質。他們想要創造出一種樂器，可以產生優美且吸引人的音色，使演奏者能夠演奏出音階上所有的音符，並把音階的範圍擴展到更高和更低的音，讓人們得以演奏更困難的音樂，而且大體說來，還要更容易吹好。

> develop (dɪˈvɛləp) *v.* 進化；進展　　improve (ɪmˈpruv) *v.* 改善
> design (dɪˈzaɪn) *n.* 設計　　shape (ʃep) *n.* 形狀
> material (məˈtɪrɪəl) *n.* 材料　　create (krɪˈet) *v.* 創造
> attractive (əˈtræktɪv) *adj.* 吸引人的　　tone (ton) *n.* 音色
> enable (ɪnˈebl̩) *v.* 使能夠　　performer (pəˈfɔrmə) *n.* 表演者
> play (ple) *n.* 演奏　　note (not) *n.* 音符　　scale (skel) *n.* 音階
> extend (ɪkˈstɛnd) *v.* 擴大　　range (rendʒ) *n.* 範圍

<u>[4](E) The remarkable way in which the modern trumpet achieves these goals is a measure of the success of all those who struggled to perfect this instrument.</u>

現代喇叭能達到這些目標，極為了不起，其之所以辦得到，在某種程度上，得歸功於所有努力改善這項樂器的人。

> remarkable (rɪ'mɑrkəbḷ) *adj.* 了不起的
> modern ('mɑdən) *adj.* 現代的　　achieve (ə'tʃiv) *v.* 達成
> goal (gol) *n.* 目標　　*a measure of* 某種程度的
> success (sək'sɛs) *n.* 成功　　struggle ('strʌgḷ) *v.* 努力
> perfect (pə'fɛkt) *v.* 使完美

The trumpet family is much more than a group of related instruments that can stir one with their sound. It is much more than narrow tubes that are capable of producing a wide variety of musical sounds. [5](C) <u>It is a link to many different periods of history and to people of many cultures.</u> From the use of trumpets in ancient religious ceremonies to the important part they play in modern rock bands, the trumpet family of instruments has much to tell us about civilization and its development.

　　喇叭家族不僅是一組用聲音來激勵人們的相關樂器。它也不僅是可以製造出各種樂聲的狹窄管子。它連繫不同時期的歷史，也連繫許多各種不同文化的人。從古代宗教儀式中使用的喇叭，到現在搖滾樂團中吃重的角色，喇叭這一家族的樂器，描繪出許多文明及其發展的過程。

> group (grup) *n.* 群；組　　related (rɪ'letɪd) *adj.* 相關的
> stir (stɝ) *v.* 鼓舞；激勵　　sound (saʊnd) *n.* 聲音
> narrow ('næro) *adj.* 狹窄的　　*be capable of* 能夠
> wide (waɪd) *adj.* 廣泛的　　*a wide variety of* 各式各樣的
> link (lɪŋk) *n.* 連繫　　period ('pɪrɪəd) *n.* 時期
> history ('hɪstrɪ) *n.* 歷史　　ancient ('enʃənt) *adj.* 古老的
> religious (rɪ'lɪdʒəs) *adj.* 宗教的　　ceremony ('sɛrə,monɪ) *n.* 儀式
> play (ple) *v.* 扮演　　*rock band* 搖滾樂團
> civilization (,sɪvḷə'zeʃən) *n.* 文明

TEST 10

說明：第 1 至 5 題，每題一個空格。請依文意在文章後所提供的 (A) 到 (E) 選項中分別選出最適當者。

Playing slow music during dinner does more than create atmosphere; ___1___. In fact, a new study suggests that the type of music you listen to while you eat may well be the key to helping you shed a few pounds or to persuading finicky kids to clean their plates.

___2___ The first meal was served in silence. One-third of the diners asked for second helpings and the meal took about 40 minutes to finish. Three weeks later researchers served the same people the same food while playing spirited tunes, such as "Stars and Stripes Forever" and "The Beer Barrel Polka." This time half of the diners asked for second helpings and ___3___.

The final meal was served ___4___. Not only did few diners ask for seconds but most of them didn't even finish their first helpings. It also took them nearly an hour to finish their meal. "Diners tarried over their food, mashing it around, cutting it up before eating it," says study leader Maria Simonson, director of the Health, Weight and Stress Clinic at Johns Hopkins. __5__ And some participants even claimed the meal tasted better.

Some appetite-soothing suggestions: waltzes, blues, and New Age music. To whet ailing appetites, try big-band tunes or rock-and-roll.

(A) they finished eating in only 31 minutes

(B) They also reported feeling fuller and more satisfied than they did after previous meals, even though they actually ate less.

(C) with slow, relaxing music, such as Mantovani and Percy Faith

(D) it actually encourages you to eat less

(E) Researchers at Johns Hopkins Medical Institution recently served three meals to 90 people.

TEST 10 詳解

Playing slow music during dinner does more than create atmosphere; [1](D) it actually encourages you to eat less.

晚餐時播放節奏緩慢的音樂，不僅能製造氣氛，其實還能使你少吃一點。

> play (ple) v. 播放　　create (krɪ'et) v. 製造
> atmosphere ('ætməs,fɪr) n. 氣氛
> actually ('æktʃuəlɪ) adv. 事實上；其實
> encourage (ɪn'kɜɪdʒ) v. 促使

In fact, a new study suggests that the type of music you listen to while you eat may well be the key to helping you shed a few pounds or to persuading finicky kids to clean their plates.

事實上，一項新的研究顯示，吃東西時所聽的音樂類型，可能會是幫助你減輕好幾磅，或是說服愛挑食的小孩，吃光盤中食物的關鍵。

> study ('stʌdɪ) n. 研究　　suggest (sə'dʒɛst) v. 暗示
> **may well** 或許；大可以　　key (ki) n. 關鍵
> shed (ʃɛd) v. 除去；擺脫　　persuade (pə'swed) v. 說服
> finicky ('fɪnɪkɪ) adj. 愛挑食的
> **clean the plate** 吃光盤中的食物

[2](E) Researchers at Johns Hopkins Medical Institution recently served three meals to 90 people. The first meal was served in silence. One-third of the diners asked for second helpings and the meal took about 40 minutes to finish.

　　約翰斯霍普金斯醫療機構的研究人員，最近提供三份餐點給九十個人。供應第一餐時是安靜無聲的。有三分之一的用餐者，要求要吃第二份，而這頓飯，花了大約四十分鐘才吃完。

> researcher (ri'sɜtʃə) *n.* 研究人員
> medical ('mɛdɪkḷ) *adj.* 醫療的
> institution (ˌɪnstə'tjuʃən) *n.* 機構
> recently ('risṇtlɪ) *adv.* 最近
> serve (sɜv) *v.* 供應　　meal (mil) *n.* 一餐
> silence ('saɪləns) *n.* 無聲；安靜
> **in silence** 安靜無聲　　**one-third** 三分之一
> diner ('daɪnə) *n.* 用餐者　　**ask for** 要求
> helping ('hɛlpɪŋ) *n.* 一份（食物）
> take (tek) *v.* 花費

Three weeks later researchers served the same people the same food while playing spirited tunes, such as "Stars and Stripes Forever" and "The Beer Barrel Polka." This time half of the diners asked for second helpings and [3](A) they finished eating in only 31 minutes.

三週後，研究人員給同一批人吃相同的食物，一邊播放輕快活潑的歌曲，像是「星條旗進行曲」及「波卡舞曲」。這一次，有一半的用餐者要求要吃第二份，而且他們在三十一分鐘之內就吃完了。

> same (sem) *adj.* 相同的
> spirited ('spɪrɪtɪd) *adj.* 活潑的
> tune (tjun) *n.* 曲調；旋律　　**such as** 像是
> stripe (straɪp) *n.* 條紋　　forever (fə'ɛvə) *adv.* 永遠
> polka ('polkə) *n.* 波卡舞曲（兩人跳的輕快舞曲）
> time (taɪm) *n.* 次　　half (hæf) *n.* 一半

The final meal was served [4](C) with slow, relaxing music, such as Mantovani and Percy Faith. Not only did few diners ask for seconds but most of them didn't even finish their first helpings. It also took them nearly an hour to finish their meal.

當供應最後一餐時，播放的是節奏緩慢、輕鬆的音樂，像是曼托瑪尼和派西費斯的曲子。不但很少用餐者要求吃第二份，而且他們大多連第一份也吃不完，他們還幾乎花了一小時才吃完那一餐。

> final ('faɪnḷ) *adj.* 最後的
> relaxing (rɪ'læksɪŋ) *adj.* 使人放鬆的
> Mantovani (ˌmæntə'vɑnɪ) *n.* (世界三大輕音樂樂團之一)
> ***Percy Faith*** 派西費斯 (輕音樂大師)
> ***not only…but also~*** 不但…而且~
> second ('sɛkənd) *n.* (食物的) 第二份
> finish ('fɪnɪʃ) *v.* 吃完　　nearly ('nɪrlɪ) *adv.* 幾乎

"Diners tarried over their food, mashing it around, cutting it up before eating it," says study leader Maria Simonson, director of the Health, Weight and Stress Clinic at Johns Hopkins.

「用餐者吃得很慢，並在吃以前將食物搗碎或切碎，」約翰霍普金斯體重與壓力診所的研究小組負責人瑪麗亞賽門森說。

> tarry ('tɛrɪ) *v.* 逗留；耽擱　　mash (mæʃ) *v.* 搗碎
> ***cut up*** 切碎　　leader ('lidɚ) *n.* 領導者
> director (də'rɛktɚ) *n.* 主任
> health (hɛlθ) *n.* 健康
> weight (wet) *n.* 體重　　stress (strɛs) *n.* 壓力
> clinic ('klɪnɪk) *n.* 診所

[5](B) They also reported feeling fuller and more satisfied than they did after previous meals, even though they actually ate less. And some participants even claimed the meal tasted better.

他們還說，覺得比吃完前兩餐覺得更飽，而且感到更滿足，雖然其實吃得比較少。而且有些參加者甚至宣稱，這一餐嚐起來更好吃。

report (rɪ'port) v. 說　　full (fʊl) adj. 飽的
satisfied ('sætɪsˌfaɪd) adj. 滿足的
previous ('privɪəs) adj. 之前的
even though 即使
participant (pɑr'tɪsəpənt) n. 參與者
claim (klem) v. 宣稱　　taste (test) v. 嚐起來

Some appetite-soothing suggestions: waltzes, blues, and New Age music. To whet ailing appetites, try big-band tunes or rock-and-roll.

　　這是一些減輕食慾的建議：華爾滋舞曲、藍調，及新世紀音樂。想刺激不好的食慾，那就試試爵士樂團的音樂，或搖滾樂。

appetite ('æpəˌtaɪt) n. 食慾
sooth (suð) v. 緩和；減輕
suggestion (sə'dʒɛstʃən) n. 建議
waltz (wɔlts) n. 華爾滋舞曲　　blues (bluz) n. pl. 藍調
New Age music 新世紀音樂
whet (hwɛt) v. 刺激；引起
ailing ('elɪŋ) adj. 狀況不佳的；生病的
big-band ('bɪgˌbænd) adj. 爵士樂團的
rock-and-roll ('rɑkən'rol) n. 搖滾樂

TEST 11

說明： 第1至5題，每題一個空格。請依文意在文章後所提供的(A)到
(E)選項中分別選出最適當者。

　　With the holiday shopping period upon us, you
can save yourself a lot of money — if you are willing
to haggle. While prices in major shopping centers
are usually fixed, you can bargain at small shops
and open markets. Here's how to get the best deal.

1. Leave the diamonds at home. Don't wear
   designer clothes and expensive jewelry
   when negotiating prices. ___1___

2. Do your homework. ___2___ If a friend or
   relative recently bought something similar,
   ask how much he paid.

3. Stay cool. Never get excited about an item.
   The moment you say, "This is great! I've
   got to have it!" the price will skyrocket.

4. Bid low. ___3___ The more time you take to increase your bid, haggling at each stage, the lower the final price will be.

5. Walk away. ___4___ If he doesn't, you can always go back.

6. Smile. If the shopkeeper sees you getting tired, he'll hold the line on his price. ___5___

(A) If the shopkeeper chases you, you should get your price.

(B) First check the fixed price of the item you want at the mall.

(C) Shopkeepers are unlikely to give you a break if you're dressed to impress.

(D) Be persistent and have fun.

(E) Offer half the asking price or less at first.

TEST 11 詳解

With the holiday shopping period upon us, you can save yourself a lot of money — if you are willing to haggle. While prices in major shopping centers are usually fixed, you can bargain at small shops and open markets. Here's how to get the best deal.

1. Leave the diamonds at home. Don't wear designer clothes and expensive jewelry when negotiating prices. **¹(C) Shopkeepers are unlikely to give you a break if you're dressed to impress.**

隨著假期購物潮的來臨，你可以為你自己省下一大筆錢——如果你願意討價還價的話。雖然大型購物中心的價格通常是不二價，但在小型商店及開放的市場中，你都可以殺價。以下教你如何得到最好的交易。

一、鑽石請擺在家裡。殺價時，千萬別穿著設計師品牌的衣服，及昂貴的珠寶。如果你穿得令人印象深刻，商店老闆是不可能給你優惠的。

upon〔ə'pɑn〕*prep.* 接近　　haggle〔'hægl〕*v.* 討價還價
fixed〔fɪkst〕*adj.* 固定的　　bargain〔'bɑrgɪn〕*v.* 討價還價
deal〔dil〕*n.* 交易　　designer〔dɪ'zaɪnɚ〕*adj.* 設計師的
jewelry〔'dʒuəlrɪ〕*n.* 珠寶　　negotiate〔nɪ'goʃɪ,et〕*v.* 談判
shopkeeper〔'ʃɑp,kipɚ〕*n.* 商店老闆
be unlikely to* + *V. 不可能
give sb. a break 饒過某人；給某人優惠
impress〔ɪm'prɛs〕*v.* 使印象深刻

2. Do your homework. **²(B) First check the fixed price of the item you want at the mall.** If a friend or relative recently bought something similar, ask how much he paid.

3. Stay cool. Never get excited about an item. The moment you say, "This is great! I've got to have it!" the price will skyrocket.

二、要作功課。先去購物中心查一下,你想要的那件物品的定價。如果你的親友最近買了類似的東西,問一下他們花多少錢買。

三、保持冷靜。絕對不要對某件物品太過興奮。當你一說出:「這個太棒了!我一定要買!」,價格就會立刻飆漲。

> ***the fixed price*** 定價　　item (ˈaɪtəm) *n.* 物品
> mall (mɔl) *n.* 購物中心　　relative (ˈrɛlətɪv) *n.* 親戚
> cool (kul) *adj.* 冷靜的　　***the moment*** 一~就 (= *as soon as*)
> ***have got to*** + *V.* 一定 (= *have to*)
> skyrocket (ˈskaɪˌrakɪt) *v.* 飆漲

4. Bid low. [3](E) Offer half the asking price or less at first.　The more time you take to increase your bid, haggling at each stage, the lower the final price will be.

5. Walk away. [4](A) If the shopkeeper chases you, you should get your price.　If he doesn't, you can always go back.

6. Smile.　If the shopkeeper sees you getting tired, he'll hold the line on his price.　[5](D) Be persistent and have fun.

四、出價要低。一開始就提出開價的一半,或更低。你花越多的時間慢慢加價,每一個階段都討價還價,你最後的成交價就會越低。

五、儘管走開。如果老板來追你,你就應該能夠以你的價錢成交。如果他沒有來追你,你總是可以再回去。

六、保持微笑。如果老板看你累了,他就會堅持他的價錢。你要堅持下去,好好享受樂趣。

> bid (bɪd) *v.* 出價　　***the asking price*** 開價
> stage (stedʒ) *n.* 階段　　chase (tʃes) *v.* 追
> ***hold the line*** 堅持　　persistent (pəˈsɪstənt) *adj.* 堅持的
> ***have fun*** 玩得愉快 (= *have a good time*)

TEST 12

說明： 第 1 至 5 題，每題一個空格。請依文意在文章後所提供的 (A) 到 (E) 選項中分別選出最適當者。

The right to free speech guaranteed by the U.S. Constitution is constantly being defended in the courts. Lately, __1__.

Two types of music are presently very popular in America: "heavy metal" and "rap." Heavy metal is a very loud and wild rock and roll music. Those who perform heavy metal are usually white men with long hair, earrings, and black leather clothes. Rap is a kind of rock and roll, but __2__. Rap musicians are usually black men with earrings and clothes that sparkle. Some people want to censor certain heavy metal and rap songs, because __3__. Many parents think children should not be exposed to such filth, and want the courts to ban the songs.

These people are usually unsuccessful in the courts, because ___4___. In fact, ___5___. However, they always have to ask the question: "If we censor one song today, what will we be asked to censor tomorrow?" In the end, it's better never to start.

(A) the judges and the juries at the trials agree that the lyrics are offensive

(B) the words are chanted rather than sung, and the music is not much more than a steady beating

(C) they are attempting to restrict the musicians' right to free speech

(D) the lyrics are sometimes obscene

(E) some people have been trying to restrict this right by censoring offensive song lyrics

TEST 12 詳解

The right to free speech guaranteed by the U.S. Constitution is constantly being defended in the courts. Lately, [1](E) some people have been trying to restrict this right by censoring offensive song lyrics.

美國憲法保障言論自由權，所以這個權利通常是受到法院保護的。最近有些人，試圖以審查不雅歌詞，來限制這項權利。

> ***right to free speech*** 言論自由權　　guarantee〔͵gærən'ti〕*v.* 保障
> constitution〔͵kɑnstə'tjuʃən〕*n.* 憲法
> constantly〔'kɑnstəntlı〕*adv.* 常常
> defend〔dı'fɛnd〕*v.* 保護　　court〔kort〕*n.* 法院
> restrict〔rı'strıkt〕*v.* 限制　　censor〔'sɛnsɚ〕*v.* 審查
> offensive〔ə'fɛnsıv〕*adj.* 令人不快的；不雅的
> lyrics〔'lırıks〕*n. pl.* 歌詞

Two types of music are presently very popular in America: "heavy metal" and "rap." Heavy metal is a very loud and wild rock and roll music. Those who perform heavy metal are usually white men with long hair, earrings, and black leather clothes. Rap is a kind of rock and roll, but [2](B) the words are chanted rather than sung, and the music is not much more than a steady beating. Rap musicians are usually black men with earrings and clothes that sparkle.

目前在美國最流行的兩種音樂型式：一為「重金屬樂」，一為「饒舌樂」。重金屬樂是一種又吵又瘋狂的搖滾樂。演奏重金屬樂的人通常是白人，他們都蓄長髮、戴耳環、一身黑皮衣打扮。饒舌也是一種搖滾樂，只是饒舌歌的歌詞是被反覆唸誦的，不是用唱的，饒舌樂只不過是有規律的節拍。饒舌歌手通常是黑人，他們也戴耳環、穿著耀眼的衣服。

presently〔'prɛzn̩tlɪ〕*adv.* 目前　　**heavy metal** 重金屬樂
rap〔ræp〕*n.* 饒舌樂　　**rock and roll** 搖滾樂
perform〔pɚ'fɔrm〕*v.* 演奏　　earring〔'ɪr,rɪŋ〕*n.* 耳環
leather〔'lɛðɚ〕*n.* 皮革　　chant〔tʃænt〕*v.* 重複地說
rather than 而不是　　**not much more than** 只不過是
steady〔'stɛdɪ〕*adj.* 有規律的　　beating〔'bitɪŋ〕*n.* 節奏
sparkle〔'spɑrkl̩〕*v.* 發亮

Some people want to censor certain heavy metal and rap songs, because [3](D) the lyrics are sometimes obscene. Many parents think children should not be exposed to such filth, and want the courts to ban the songs.

有些人希望能審查某些重金屬和饒舌歌，因爲這些歌的歌詞有時有點下流。許多父母都認爲，小孩子不應該接觸這種低級的玩意兒，他們希望法院能禁止這些歌曲的播放。

　　　　obscene〔əb'sin〕*adj.* 下流的　　**be exposed to** 接觸
　　　　filth〔fɪlθ〕*n.* 下流的東西　　ban〔bæn〕*v.* 禁止

These people are usually unsuccessful in the courts, because [4](C) they are attempting to restrict the musicians' right to free speech. In fact, [5](A) the judges and the juries at the trials agree that the lyrics are offensive. However, they always have to ask the question: "If we censor one song today, what will we be asked to censor tomorrow?" In the end, it's better never to start.

　　然而，這些人在法院，通常是不會成功的，因爲他們這麼做，是企圖要限制音樂人的言論自由。事實上，法官和陪審團在判決時，都同意這些歌詞相當不雅。然而他們總是必須問這個問題：如果我們今天審查一首歌，明天會被要求審查什麼東西呢？最後，這種事最好還是少碰爲妙。

　　　　attempt〔ə'tɛmpt〕*v.* 企圖　　judge〔dʒʌdʒ〕*n.* 法官
　　　　jury〔'dʒʊrɪ〕*n.* 陪審團　　trial〔'traɪəl〕*n.* 審判

TEST 13

If you've ever had the misfortune of breaking a bone, you've probably been told, "When the bone does heal, it will be stronger than before."　　1　　 Well, like a lot of other pearls of folk wisdom, this one isn't quite true. But it is true that your body does a marvelous job of healing and broken bones do knit quite nicely.　　2　　 When you break a bone, mending begins immediately. Blood cells rush to the site of the fracture and form a gelatinous substance around the bone's broken ends, holding them together like a scab holds together pieces of torn skin.

In a few days, this so-called fracture callus is established and the body starts to manufacture new bone cells and blood vessels.　　3　　 A doctor should align and set a broken bone before the callus has developed. Usually this means putting your broken body part in a cast or splint. ___4___ You'll heal in about six to eight weeks, depending on what you broke and how bad the break was.

___5___ If you're not careful, you can break the same bone again.

(A) Immobility is crucial for the bone to heal in the right shape.

(B) A bone heals itself much the same way your skin heals itself when you get a cut.

(C) Is that true?

(D) But the process won't turn you into the Man of Steel.

(E) This transforms the callus into bone much the same way the scab on your knee is turned into skin.

TEST 13 詳解

If you've ever had the misfortune of breaking a bone, you've probably been told, "When the bone does heal, it will be stronger than before." [1](C) Is that true?

如果你曾經很不幸地骨折，可能會有人跟你說：「當骨頭真的癒合時，會比以前更強壯。」是真的嗎？

> ever ('ɛvə) *adv.* 曾經
> misfortune (mɪs'fɔrtʃən) *n.* 不幸
> **break a bone** 骨折　　heal (hil) *v.* 癒合

Well, like a lot of other pearls of folk wisdom, this one isn't quite true. But it is true that your body does a marvelous job of healing and broken bones do knit quite nicely.

嗯，就像許多其他的民間智慧一樣，這種說法也不是很正確。但是身體真的會進行很神奇的癒合工作，而且折斷的骨頭真的能癒合得很好。

> **pearls of folk wisdom** 民間的智慧
> marvelous ('marvləs) *adj.* 神奇的
> knit (nɪt) *v.* 接合；癒合 (= *heal* = *mend*)
> quite (kwaɪt) *adv.* 相當
> nicely ('naɪslɪ) *adv.* 很好地

[2](B) A bone heals itself much the same way your skin heals itself when you get a cut. When you break a bone, mending begins immediately.

骨頭癒合的方式，非常像當你有傷口時，皮膚癒合的方式。當你骨折時，
癒合的工作會立刻開始進行。

> skin〔skɪn〕*n.* 皮膚
> A bone…much the same way your…
> = A bone…*in* much the same way *as* your…
> ***much the same*** 非常像   cut〔kʌt〕*n.* 傷口
> mending〔'mɛndɪŋ〕*n.* 癒合 (= *healing*)
> immediately〔ɪ'midɪɪtlɪ〕*adv.* 立即

Blood cells rush to the site of the fracture and form a gelatinous
substance around the bone's broken ends, holding them together
like a scab holds together pieces of torn skin.

血球會很快前往骨折的部位，在斷骨末端的周圍，形成膠狀的物質，使
斷骨連接在一起，就像是痂會連接好幾片被撕裂的皮膚一樣。

> cell〔sɛl〕*n.* 細胞
> ***blood cell*** 血球   ***rush to*** 衝往
> site〔saɪt〕*n.* 部位
> fracture〔'fræktʃɚ〕*n.* 骨折
> gelatinous〔dʒə'lætṇˏəs〕*adj.* 膠狀的
> substance〔'sʌbstəns〕*n.* 物質   end〔ɛnd〕*n.* 末端
> ***hold~together*** 使~連接在一起
> scab〔skæb〕*n.* 痂   piece〔pis〕*n.* 片；塊
> torn〔tɔrn〕*adj.* 被撕裂的

In a few days, this so-called fracture callus is established and the body starts to manufacture new bone cells and blood vessels.

過了幾天之後，這個所謂的骨折癒合組織就形成了，人體也會開始製造新的骨細胞和血管。

> so-called〔'so'kɔld〕*adj.* 所謂的
> callus〔'kæləs〕*n.* 繭；癒合組織
> establish〔ə'stæblɪʃ〕*v.* 形成
> manufacture〔ˌmænjə'fæktʃə〕*v.* 製造
> vessel〔'vɛsl̩〕*n.* 血管（= blood vessel）

[3](E) This transforms the callus into bone much the same way the scab on your knee is turned into skin.

這會使癒合組織轉變爲骨頭，和你膝蓋上的痂，轉變爲皮膚的過程，非常相像。

> transform〔træns'fɔrm〕*v.* 使轉變
> knee〔ni〕*n.* 膝蓋　　**turn into** 變成

A doctor should align and set a broken bone before the callus has developed. Usually this means putting your broken body part in a cast or splint. [4](A) Immobility is crucial for the bone to heal in the right shape.

醫生應該在癒合組織形成前，就使斷掉的骨頭成一直線，並且使斷骨復位。通常這就表示，要把身體折斷的部位，敷上石膏，或裝上夾板。要讓骨頭以正確的形狀癒合，固定不動是非常重要的。

align〔əˋlaɪn〕*v.* 使成一直線；使（斷骨）復位
set a broken bone 使斷骨復位
develop〔dɪˋvɛləp〕*v.* 形成
part〔part〕*n.* 部位　　cast〔kæst〕*n.* 石膏
splint〔splɪnt〕*n.* 夾板
immobility〔͵ɪmoˋbɪlətɪ〕*n.* 固定不動
crucial〔ˋkruʃəl〕*adj.* 非常重要的
shape〔ʃep〕*n.* 形狀　　***in ~ shape*** 以 ~ 形狀

You'll heal in about six to eight weeks, depending on what you broke and how bad the break was.

骨頭再過大約六至八週就會癒合，這要視骨折的部位，以及骨折的情況有多嚴重而定。

> ***depend on*** 視 ~ 而定
> bad〔bæd〕*adj.* 嚴重的　　break〔brek〕*n.* 骨折情況

[5](D) But the process won't turn you into the Man of Steel. If you're not careful, you can break the same bone again.

但是這個過程不會使你變成超人。如果你不小心，同樣的部位可能還會再次骨折。

> process〔ˋprasɛs〕*n.* 過程　　steel〔stil〕*n.* 鋼
> ***the Man of Steel*** 超人

TEST 14

說明： 第 1 至 5 題，每題一個空格。請依文意在文章後所提供的 (A) 到 (E) 選項中分別選出最適當者。

　　In pioneer days, neighbors were very important. They helped one another raise a house, build a barn, and clear fields. Families depended on one another for friendship and entertainment. ___1___ A family may not even know the other families that live close by.

　　Many people now depend on machines instead of on their neighbors. ___2___ Today, families stay inside with their automatic dryers, and can't hear anything above the roar of their power lawn mowers. The children are inside watching their favorite TV show.

　　Is the idea of being neighborly old-fashioned? ___3___ Suddenly, everyone shared the same problem, and our largest city became a group of eight million neighbors. People with cars offered rides to those walking. ___4___ Trapped in elevators, people played word games and helped keep each other in good spirits.

In times of trouble, people still depend on one another. ___5___

(A) Other persons helped direct traffic.

(B) But today in our cities and suburbs, neighboring is not common.

(C) As time goes on, people may once again feel that being a good neighbor is important.

(D) In our grandparents' time, women met while they hung out the washing, and men stopped and talked while they mowed the lawns.

(E) In 1965, a power failure hit New York City, and many thousands of people were left stranded.

TEST 14 詳解

In pioneer days, neighbors were very important. They helped one another raise a house, build a barn, and clear fields. Families depended on one another for friendship and entertainment. [1](B) But today in our cities and suburbs, neighboring is not common. A family may not even know the other families that live close by.

在拓荒時代，鄰居是非常重要的。他們彼此互相幫忙蓋房子、建穀倉，以及開墾農地。每戶人家都像朋友一樣相互依賴，並共同玩樂。可是在現今的城市和郊區裡，敦親睦鄰已經不普遍了。許多家庭甚至於不認識住在附近的人家。

pioneer (ˌpaɪəˈnɪr) *adj.* 拓荒時期的　　***one another*** 互相
raise (rez) *v.* 建立　　barn (barn) *n.* 穀倉
clear (klɪr) *v.* 開墾　　field (fild) *n.* 田地
depend on 依賴　　entertainment (ˌɛntɚˈtenmənt) *n.* 娛樂
suburbs (ˈsʌbɝbz) *n. pl.* 郊區
neighboring (ˈnebərɪŋ) *n.* 做鄰居；敦親睦鄰

Many people now depend on machines instead of on their neighbors. [2](D) In our grandparents' time, women met while they hung out the washing, and men stopped and talked while they mowed the lawns. Today, families stay inside with their automatic dryers, and can't hear anything above the roar of their power lawn mowers. The children are inside watching their favorite TV show.

現代人都是靠機器，而不靠鄰居了。在我們祖父母的時代，女人總是在晾衣服時聚在一起，而男人都會在修剪草坪時，停下來聊天。現代的家庭，都是在屋內使用自動烘乾機，而且除了電動割草機的轟隆作響聲之外，聽不到任何聲音。小孩子也都窩在屋內，看他們最喜愛的電視節目。

instead of 而不是　　***hang out*** 將（衣服）晾在外面
washing〔'wɑʃɪŋ〕*n.* 洗滌物　　mow〔mo〕*v.* 收割
lawn〔lɔn〕*n.* 草坪　　automatic〔ˌɔtə'mætɪk〕*adj.* 自動的
dryer〔'draɪə〕*n.* 烘乾機　　roar〔ror〕*n.*（機器發出的）隆隆聲
power〔'pauə〕*adj.* 電動的　　***lawn mower*** 割草機

Is the idea of being neighborly old-fashioned? [3](E) In 1965, a power failure hit New York City, and many thousands of people were left stranded. Suddenly, everyone shared the same problem, and our largest city became a group of eight million neighbors. People with cars offered rides to those walking. [4](A) Other persons helped direct traffic. Trapped in elevators, people played word games and helped keep each other in good spirits.

　　難道這種敦親睦鄰的觀念落伍了嗎？在一九六五年，紐約市發生了一場大停電，數千名的民眾因此被困住，動彈不得。突然間大家都有同樣的問題，這使得居住在這個全美第一大城的八百萬人口，都變成好鄰居。有車的人讓走路的人搭便車，其他的人幫忙指揮交通。被困在電梯裡的人，一起玩猜字遊戲，並彼此互相加油打氣。

neighborly〔'nebəlɪ〕*adj.* 和睦的
old-fashioned〔'old'fæʃənd〕*adj.* 過時的　　***power failure*** 停電
hit〔hɪt〕*v.* 襲擊　　stranded〔'strændɪd〕*adj.* 進退兩難的
direct〔də'rɛkt〕*v.* 指揮　　trap〔træp〕*v.* 把～關進
word game 猜字遊戲　　***in good spirits*** 心情好

In times of trouble, people still depend on one another. [5](C) As time goes on, people may once again feel that being a good neighbor is important.

　　有難的時候，人們仍是會互相幫忙的。隨著時間的過去，人們可能會再次感覺到，當一個好鄰居是非常重要的。

in times of 在～的時候　　***go on***（時間）過去

TEST 15

說明： 第1至5題，每題一個空格。請依文意在文章後所提供的(A)到
(E) 選項中分別選出最適當者。

    Stalking is a common problem among
Hollywood stars, but ___1___. Many victims are
pursued and pestered for years by spurned lovers.

    Aid organizations estimate that ___2___. In
Los Angeles, home to many of the famous, the
LAPD has set up a special department to fight
stalking. Anti-stalking laws have been in place in
every U.S. state since the early 1990s.

    Michael Newall, founding director of the aid
organization Stalking Rescue says ___3___, usually
in combination with low self-esteem. They are
most often men who do not understand that their
excessive love can be threatening. For example,
___4___: "Either you marry me or I cut your throat,"
wrote a man who was caught three times on the
star's property and is now serving a jail sentence.

On the other hand, female stalkers are often

schizophrenics, who really consider themselves

life partners of their victims. Hollywood star

___5___, the climax of a three-year bombardment

of gifts and letters to him.

(A) 1.4 million Americans suffer from such

harassment from unwanted admirers

(B) Madonna was subjected to an aggressive

form of stalking

(C) Brad Pitt last year found a 19-year-old

woman in his bed at his Malibu villa

(D) it is a crime that increasingly affects

ordinary people, too

(E) most stalkers suffer from serious

personality defects

TEST 15 詳解

Stalking is a common problem among Hollywood stars, but
[1](D) it is a crime that increasingly affects ordinary people, too.
Many victims are pursued and pestered for years by spurned lovers.

好萊塢明星被跟蹤的問題屢見不鮮,但是這種犯罪行為,現在也逐漸影響到一般人。許多受害者,都是常年被分手的愛人糾纏及騷擾。

> stalking ('stɔkɪŋ) n. 跟蹤   common ('kɑmən) adj. 常見的
> Hollywood ('hɑlɪ,wʊd) n. 好萊塢
> crime (kraɪm) n. 犯罪
> increasingly (ɪn'krisɪŋlɪ) adv. 逐漸   affect (ə'fɛkt) v. 影響
> ordinary ('ɔrdn̩,ɛrɪ) adj. 普通的
> victim ('vɪktɪm) n. 受害者   pursue (pɚ'su) v. 糾纏
> pester ('pɛstɚ) v. 困擾   spurned (spɝnd) adj. 分手的

Aid organizations estimate that [2](A) 1.4 million Americans
suffer from such harassment from unwanted admirers. In Los
Angeles, home to many of the famous, the LAPD has set up a
special department to fight stalking. Anti-stalking laws have been
in place in every U.S. state since the early 1990s.

救援機構估計,大約有一百四十萬個美國人,正被惱人的愛慕者所騷擾。由於有許多名人住在洛杉磯,洛杉磯警局特別成立一個部門,要來打擊這種跟蹤行為。自一九九〇年代初期,美國各州就已經開始實施反跟蹤法了。

> aid (ed) n. 救援   organization (,ɔrgənə'zeʃən) n. 機構
> estimate ('ɛstə,met) v. 估計   *suffer from* 遭受 (痛苦)
> harassment (hə'ræsmənt) n. 騷擾
> unwanted (ʌn'wɑntɪd) adj. 不受歡迎的
> admirer (əd'maɪrɚ) n. 愛慕者   *the famous* 名人
> *LAPD* 洛杉磯市警局   *set up* 設立

department〔dɪ'pɑrtmənt〕*n.* 部門
fight〔faɪt〕*v.* 和～作戰;對抗
anti-〔'æntaɪ ; 'æntɪ〕*adj.* 反～的　　***in place*** 就位;實施的

Michael Newall, founding director of the aid organization Stalking Rescue says [3](E) most stalkers suffer from serious personality defects, usually in combination with low self-esteem. They are most often men who do not understand that their excessive love can be threatening.

麥可紐沃,是「跟蹤營救」這家救援機構的創辦人,他說大部分的跟蹤者,都有嚴重的人格缺陷,通常自尊心極低。這些人都不知道,過度的愛慕之意,是具有威脅性的。

founding〔'faʊndɪŋ〕*adj.* 創始的
director〔də'rɛktɚ〕*n.* 指導者　　***founding director*** 創辦人
rescue〔'rɛskju〕*n.* 救援　　stalker〔'stɔkɚ〕*n.* 跟蹤者
serious〔'sɪrɪəs〕*adj.* 嚴重的　　personality〔ˌpɝsn̩'ælətɪ〕*n.* 人格
defect〔'difɛkt〕*n.* 缺陷　　***in combination with*** 與～結合
self-esteem〔'sɛlfəs'tim〕*n.* 自尊
excessive〔ɪk'sɛsɪv〕*adj.* 過度的
threatening〔'θrɛtn̩ɪŋ〕*adj.* 威脅的

For example, [4](B) Madonna was subjected to an aggressive form of stalking: "Either you marry me or I cut your throat," wrote a man who was caught three times on the star's property and is now serving a jail sentence.

舉例來說,瑪丹娜就曾遭遇一種侵犯式的跟蹤:一名男子在寫給她的信上說,「嫁給我,要不然我就殺了妳」,這名男子因為非法進入瑪丹娜的私人土地,已經三度被捕,目前正在監獄服刑中。

subject〔səb'dʒɛkt〕*v.* 使遭受；使遭遇
be subjected to 遭受；被
aggressive〔ə'grɛsɪv〕*adj.* 侵犯的　　form〔fɔrm〕*n.* 形式
marry〔'mærɪ〕*v.* 結婚　　throat〔θrot〕*n.* 喉嚨
property〔'prɑpətɪ〕*n.* 土地　　sentence〔'sɛntəns〕*n.* 刑罰
serve〔sɝv〕*v.* 服（刑）　　jail〔dʒel〕*n.* 監獄
serve a jail sentence 坐牢

On the other hand, female stalkers are often schizophrenics, who really consider themselves life partners of their victims.

另一方面，女性跟蹤者通常是精神分裂症患者，她們把自己當成是這些被跟蹤者的終身伴侶。

on the other hand 另一方面
female〔'fimel〕*adj.* 女性的
schizophrenic〔ˌskɪzə'frɛnɪk〕*n.* 精神分裂症患者
consider〔kən'sɪdə〕*v.* 視為
life partner 終身伴侶

Hollywood star [5](C) Brad Pitt last year found a 19-year-old woman in his bed at his Malibu villa, the climax of a three-year bombardment of gifts and letters to him.

好萊塢大明星布萊德彼特，去年在他的馬里布海灘別墅，發現一位十九歲的女孩躺在他床上，這是整個跟蹤行為的最高潮，因為那個女孩三年來，一直大量送禮物和情書轟炸這位大明星。

villa〔'vɪlə〕*n.* 別墅
climax〔'klaɪmæks〕*n.* 最高潮
bombardment〔bɑm'bɑrdmənt〕*n.* 轟炸

TEST 16

說明： 第 1 至 5 題，每題一個空格。請依文意在文章後所提供的(A)到
(E) 選項中分別選出最適當者。

Three hundred years after the African slave trade began,
European humanists began to write pamphlets opposing
slavery. Convinced that slavery was immoral, ___1___.

Finally, Britain prohibited the trade in 1807, ___2___, and
other European nations soon followed. Yet, because slavery
was still legal in many countries and it rolled in money for the
traders, ___3___. A number of African kings who had grown
dependent on profits from the trade also cooperated with the
West in keeping the trade going.

Increasing British efforts against both European and
African slave traders gradually choked off the export of slaves
from western Africa. As this was happening, however, ___4___.
Also, the centuries-old slave trade with the Arab countries
continued in the 19th century. Not until 1870, when slavery was
made illegal everywhere in America and Europe, ___5___.

(A) the slaves from eastern Africa were on the increase

(B) did the African slave trade come to an end

(C) they worked hard to end the trade

(D) the trade continued

(E) the United States did likewise in 1808

TEST 16 詳解

Three hundred years after the African slave trade began,
European humanists began to write pamphlets opposing slavery.
Convinced that slavery was immoral, [1](C) they worked hard to end
the trade.

在非洲開始買賣奴隸後三百年，歐洲的人道主義者，開始寫一些小
冊子，反對奴隸制度。他們相信奴隸制度是不道德的，所以非常努力，
想結束這樣的貿易行為。

> slave〔slev〕*n.* 奴隸　　trade〔tred〕*n.* 交易；買賣
> European〔͵jurə'piən〕*adj.* 歐洲的
> humanist〔'hjumənɪst〕*n.* 人道主義者
> pamphlet〔'pæmflɪt〕*n.* 小冊子　　oppose〔ə'poz〕*v.* 反對
> slavery〔'slevərɪ〕*n.* 奴隸制度
> convince〔kən'vɪns〕*v.* 使相信
> immoral〔ɪ'mɔrəl〕*adj.* 不道德的

Finally, Britain prohibited the trade in 1807, [2](E) the United
States did likewise in 1808, and other European nations soon
followed. Yet, because slavery was still legal in many countries and
it rolled in money for the traders, [3](D) the trade continued. A number
of African kings who had grown dependent on profits from the trade
also cooperated with the West in keeping the trade going.

最後，在一八○七年，英國禁止了奴隸買賣，一八○八年，美國也
跟進，很快地，歐洲其他國家也照做。然而，因為奴隸制度在許多國家，
仍然是合法的，而且可以為商人帶來大筆財富，所以這項買賣還是持續
進行。有一些非洲國王，因為非常依賴這項買賣所得到的利潤，所以也
和西方一起合作，使得這項貿易繼續下去。

prohibit〔proˈhɪbɪt〕*v.* 禁止　　likewise〔ˈlaɪk,waɪz〕*adv.* 同樣地
legal〔ˈligl̩〕*adj.* 合法的　　***roll in***（錢）滾滾而來
trader〔ˈtredɚ〕*n.* 商人　　continue〔kənˈtɪnju〕*v.* **繼續；持續**
dependent〔dɪˈpɛndənt〕*adj.* 依賴的 < *on* >
profit〔ˈprɑfɪt〕*n.* 利潤　　cooperate〔koˈɑpə,ret〕*v.* 合作

Increasing British efforts against both European and African
slave traders gradually choked off the export of slaves from western
Africa.　As this was happening, however, [4](A) the slaves from eastern
Africa were on the increase.

　　越來越多的英國人，努力反對歐洲和非洲的奴隸買賣，逐漸地終止
了西非奴隸的出口。然而，在發生這件事的同時，來自東非的奴隸卻在
增加當中。

increasing〔ɪnˈkrisɪŋ〕*adj.* 越來越多的（= *more and more*）
against〔əˈgɛnst〕*prep.* 反對　　***choke off*** 使終止
export〔ˈɛksport〕*n.* 出口
on the increase 增加中（= *increasing*）

Also, the centuries-old slave trade with the Arab countries
continued in the 19th century.　Not until 1870, when slavery was
made illegal everywhere in America and Europe, [5](B) did the African
slave trade come to an end.

此外，與阿拉伯國家數百年來的奴隸買賣，也持續到十九世紀。直到一
八七〇年，奴隸制度在美洲及歐洲各地，都被宣布不合法時，非洲的奴
隸買賣才總算結束了。

Arab〔ˈærəb〕*adj.* 阿拉伯的　　illegal〔ɪˈligl̩〕*adj.* 不合法的
come to an end 結束；停止（= *end*）

TEST 17

說明： 第 1 至 5 題，每題一個空格。請依文意在文章後所提供的 (A) 到 (E) 選項中分別選出最適當者。

_____1_____ The virus slowly destroys the body's immune system, leaving the person increasingly defenseless against other infections and some cancers.

AIDS is primarily a sexually transmitted disease. _____2_____ At highest risk are people who have many sexual partners. _____3_____ Transfusion of HIV-contaminated blood can infect the person receiving it. However, an increasing number of countries systematically screen and reject blood containing HIV antibodies.

_____4_____ People who inject illegal drugs are at high risk because many of them share unclean needles and syringes. But any unsterilized skin-piercing instrument, including ear-piercing or tattoo needles, can spread the virus.

_____5_____ Worldwide, HIV-infected mothers face on average a one-in-four chance of having an infected baby, and most babies born with the virus die before they are five years old. If the mother has been infected recently, she may also transmit the virus through breast-feeding.

(A) The use of shared needles may also lead to AIDS infection.

(B) AIDS is the last stage of the infection caused by HIV, the human immunodeficiency virus.

(C) Finally, a woman infected with HIV can pass the virus on to her baby during pregnancy, during birth or shortly after birth.

(D) Blood is another means by which AIDS may be transmitted.

(E) Transmission can occur from man to woman, man to man, or woman to man.

TEST 17 詳解

[1](B) AIDS is the last stage of the infection caused by HIV, the human immunodeficiency virus.

 愛滋病是感染愛滋病毒的最後一個階段，而愛滋病毒即人體免疫缺乏病毒。

> stage〔sted3〕*n.* 階段
> infection〔ɪnˈfɛkʃən〕*n.* 感染；傳染病
> *HIV* 愛滋病病毒（= *human immunodeficiency virus*）
> immunodeficiency〔ˌɪmjunodɪˈfɪʃənsɪ〕*n.* 免疫不全
> virus〔ˈvaɪrəs〕*n.* 病毒

The virus slowly destroys the body's immune system, leaving the person increasingly defenseless against other infections and some cancers.

愛滋病毒會慢慢破壞人體的免疫系統，使人愈來愈無法抵抗其他的傳染病，與某些癌症。

> destroy〔dɪˈstrɔɪ〕*v.* 破壞
> immune〔ɪˈmjun〕*adj.* 免疫的
> *immune system* 免疫系統
> leave〔liv〕*v.* 使
> increasingly〔ɪnˈkrisɪŋlɪ〕*adv.* 愈來愈
> defenseless〔dɪˈfɛnslɪs〕*adj.* 無防衛能力的
> cancer〔ˈkænsɚ〕*n.* 癌症

AIDS is primarily a sexually transmitted disease. [2](E) Transmission can occur from man to woman, man to man, or woman to man. At highest risk are people who have many sexual partners.

愛滋病主要是經由性行爲而傳染的疾病。可能發生的傳染途徑有，男生傳給女生，男生傳給男生，或女生傳給男生。有許多性伴侶的人，是愛滋病的高危險群。

primarily ('praɪ,mɛrəlɪ) *adv.* 主要地
sexually ('sɛkʃuəlɪ) *adv.* 經由性行爲地
transmit (træns'mɪt) *v.* 傳染　　disease (dɪ'ziz) *n.* 疾病
be at risk 有危險　　***sexual partner*** 性伴侶

[3](D) Blood is another means by which AIDS may be transmitted. Transfusion of HIV-contaminated blood can infect the person receiving it.

血液是另一個可能傳染愛滋病的途徑。輸的血液如果被愛滋病毒感染，就會傳染接受輸血的人。

blood (blʌd) *n.* 血　　means (minz) *n.* 途徑；方法
transfusion (træns'fjuʒən) *n.* 輸血
contaminate (kən'tæmə,net) *v.* 污染
infect (ɪn'fɛkt) *v.* 感染
receive (rɪ'siv) *v.* 接受；得到

However, an increasing number of countries systematically screen and reject blood containing HIV antibodies.

不過，有愈來愈多的國家，會有系統地篩檢，並拒絕接受含有愛滋病毒抗體的血液。

> increasing〔 ɪn'krisɪŋ 〕adj. 愈來愈多的
> number〔 'nʌmbɚ 〕n. 數量
> systematically〔 ,sɪstə'mætɪklɪ 〕adv. 有系統地
> screen〔 skrin 〕v. 篩檢　　reject〔 rɪ'dʒɛkt 〕v. 拒絕接受
> contain〔 kən'ten 〕v. 包含　　antibody〔 'æntɪ,bɑdɪ 〕n. 抗體

[4](A) The use of shared needles may also lead to AIDS infection. People who inject illegal drugs are at high risk because many of them share unclean needles and syringes.

　　共用針頭可能也會導致感染愛滋病。注射毒品的人，是高危險群，因為他們當中有很多人，會共用不乾淨的針頭及注射筒。

> shared〔 ʃɛrd 〕adj. 共用的　　needle〔 'nidl̩ 〕n. 針頭
> **lead to** 造成；導致　　inject〔 ɪn'dʒɛkt 〕v. 注射
> illegal〔 ɪ'ligl̩ 〕adj. 非法的　　**illegal drugs** 毒品
> share〔 ʃɛr 〕v. 共用　　syringe〔 'sɪrɪndʒ 〕n. 注射筒

But any unsterilized skin-piercing instrument, including ear-piercing or tattoo needles, can spread the virus.
但是任何未消毒的刺穿皮膚的用具，包括穿耳洞或刺青的針，都會散播病毒。

> unsterilized〔 ʌn'stɛrə,laɪzd 〕adj. 未消毒的
> pierce〔 pɪrs 〕v. 刺穿
> instrument〔 'ɪnstrəmənt 〕n. 器具；工具
> tattoo〔 tæ'tu 〕n. 刺青　　spread〔 sprɛd 〕v. 散播

[5](C) Finally, a woman infected with HIV can pass the virus on to her baby during pregnancy, during birth or shortly after birth.

最後，感染到愛滋病毒的婦女，可能會在懷孕、生產期間，或嬰兒出生後不久，將病毒傳給嬰兒。

> ***pass ~ on to*** 把～傳給
> pregnancy ('prɛgnənsɪ) *n.* 懷孕
> shortly ('ʃɔrtlɪ) *adv.* 不久

Worldwide, HIV-infected mothers face on average a one-in-four chance of having an infected baby, and most babies born with the virus die before they are five years old.

在全世界，感染愛滋病毒的母親，平均而言，有四分之一的可能性，會生下受感染的嬰兒，而大多數一出生就有愛滋病的嬰兒，在五歲之前就會死亡。

> worldwide ('wɝld'waɪd) *adv.* 在全世界
> face (fes) *v.* 面臨　　***on average*** 平均而言
> ***one-in-four*** *adj.* 四分之一的
> ***have a baby*** 生小孩

If the mother has been infected recently, she may also transmit the virus through breast-feeding.

如果母親是最近才被感染，她也有可能會經由哺乳，把愛滋病毒傳染給孩子。

> recently ('risn̩tlɪ) *adv.* 最近
> breast-feeding ('brɛst͵fidɪŋ) *n.* 餵奶；哺乳

TEST 18

The complex relationship between the Sun and the Earth results in considerable changes in the world's weather over long periods of time. ___1___ Since the industrial revolution, carbon dioxide emissions have increased so much that they are beginning to have an influence on the earth's climate. ___2___ It means that the temperatures in the atmosphere are increasing rapidly. The result of this is that the ice caps at the North and South Poles are beginning to melt. ___3___ Millions of human beings and animals living in lowland areas will be threatened.

____4____ The Inuit have lived in the frozen wastes of the North Pole for thousands of years, and nomadic peoples of the great deserts survive in the searing heat. ____5____ Or we might face the danger that the damage might soon threaten the existence of all life on this planet.

(A) Human beings are able to survive in some of the most extreme weather conditions on Earth.

(B) We are now faced with a phenomenon called global warming.

(C) Thus, the ocean levels will rise and coastal areas will become flooded.

(D) However, it's time for mankind to do something to halt the global warming.

(E) Today, the activities of man have become an important element in this equation.

TEST 18 詳解

The complex relationship between the Sun and the Earth results in considerable changes in the world's weather over long periods of time. [1](E) Today, the activities of man have become an important element in this equation.

長久以來，太陽與地球之間複雜的關係，導致了全球天氣相當大的變化。今日人類的活動，已經變成這個方程式中相當重要的因素。

complex〔'kɑmplɛks〕 adj. 複雜的
relationship〔rɪ'leʃən,ʃɪp〕 n. 關係
result in 導致　　considerable〔kən'sɪdərəbḷ〕 adj. 相當大的
period〔'pɪrɪəd〕 n. 時期　　element〔'ɛləmənt〕 n. 因素
equation〔ɪ'kweʃən〕 n. 方程式

Since the industrial revolution, carbon dioxide emissions have increased so much that they are beginning to have an influence on the earth's climate. [2](B) We are now faced with a phenomenon called global warming.

自從工業革命之後，排出的二氧化碳增加很多，以致於它們開始對地球的氣候產生影響。我們現在正面臨一種現象，叫做全球暖化。

industrial〔ɪn'dʌstrɪəl〕 adj. 工業的
revolution〔,rɛvə'luʃən〕 n. 革命　　carbon〔'kɑrbən〕 n. 碳
dioxide〔daɪ'ɑksaɪd〕 n. 二氧化物　　**carbon dioxide** 二氧化碳
emission〔ɪ'mɪʃən〕 n. 排放
increase〔ɪn'kris〕 v. 增加　　influence〔'ɪnfluəns〕 n. 影響
climate〔'klaɪmɪt〕 n. 氣候　　**be faced with** 面對
phenomenon〔fə'nɑmə,nɑn〕 n. 現象
global〔'globḷ〕 adj. 全球的　　**global warming** 全球暖化

It means that the temperatures in the atmosphere are increasing rapidly. The result of this is that the ice caps at the North and South Poles are beginning to melt.

全球暖化即大氣的溫度快速地上升。這樣的結果是，北極和南極的冰帽開始融化。

  mean〔min〕v. 意謂著；意思是
  temperature〔'tɛmpərətʃɚ〕n. 溫度
  atmosphere〔'ætməs,fɪr〕n. 大氣
  rapidly〔'ræpɪdlɪ〕adv. 迅速地
  result〔rɪ'zʌlt〕n. 結果 cap〔kæp〕n. 帽子
  ice cap 冰帽 north〔nɔrθ〕adj. 北的
  south〔sauθ〕adj. 南的 pole〔pol〕n. 極地
  the North and South Poles 南北極
  melt〔mɛlt〕v. 融化

[3](C) Thus, the ocean levels will rise and coastal areas will become flooded. Millions of human beings and animals living in lowland areas will be threatened.

因此，海平面會上升，沿岸地區將被淹沒。數以百萬住在低窪地區的人及動物將受到威脅。

  thus〔ðʌs〕adv. 因此 level〔'lɛvl̩〕n. 水平面；平面
  ocean level 海平面（ = *sea level* ）
  rise〔raɪz〕v. 上升 coastal〔'kostl̩〕adj. 海岸的
  area〔'ɛrɪə〕n. 地區 flood〔flʌd〕v. 淹水
  million〔'mɪljən〕n. 百萬
  human being 人類 lowland〔'lo,lænd〕adj. 低地的
  threaten〔'θrɛtn̩〕v. 威脅

⁴(A) <u>Human beings are able to survive in some of the most
extreme weather conditions on Earth.</u> The Inuit have lived in the
frozen wastes of the North Pole for thousands of years, and
nomadic peoples of the great deserts survive in the searing heat.

人類可以在地球上最惡劣的天氣下生存。數千年以來，因紐人住在
北極結冰的荒地裡，而大沙漠的遊牧民族則生活在炙熱當中裡。

survive〔 sə'vaɪv 〕v. 生存

extreme〔 ɪk'strim 〕adj. 極端的；極惡劣的

condition〔 kən'dɪʃən 〕n. 情況

Inuit〔'ɪnjuət 〕n. 因紐人（即愛斯基摩人）

frozen〔'frozn̩ 〕adj. 冰凍的

wastes〔 wests 〕n. pl. 荒野；荒地

nomadic〔 no'mædɪk 〕adj. 游牧的　　people〔'pipl̩ 〕n. 民族

desert〔'dɛzət 〕n. 沙漠　　searing〔'sɪrɪŋ 〕adj. 炙熱的

heat〔 hit 〕n. 熱；高溫

⁵(D) <u>However, it's time for mankind to do something to halt the
global warming.</u> Or we might face the danger that the damage
might soon threaten the existence of all life on this planet.

然而，現在是人類該做點事，來阻止全球暖化的時候了。否則我們可能
會面臨一個危機，就是全球暖化所帶來的損害，很快就會威脅到地球上
所有生物的生存。

mankind〔 mæn'kaɪnd 〕n. 人類　　halt〔 hɔlt 〕v. 停止

danger〔'dendʒə 〕n. 危險；危機

damage〔'dæmɪdʒ 〕n. 傷害　　existence〔 ɪg'zɪstəns 〕n. 生存

planet〔'plænɪt 〕n. 行星

TEST 19

說明：第 1 至 5 題，每題一個空格。請依文意在文章後所提供的 (A) 到
(E) 選項中分別選出最適當者。

Do you compulsively surf the Web when you should be
eating or sleeping? Such behavior has aroused the interest of
psychologists. ___1___ They can only say that it is a new and
fascinating field waiting to be explored.

___2___ An "Internet Addict" is described as anyone who
spends up to 38 hours per week on-line for non-work purposes.

___3___ Students may also be at risk. One third of students know
someone with social or academic problems which are traceable
to heavy Net use.

___4___ Others see the Net as something that drives human
beings to overdo. ___5___ We need more comprehensive
research before pathological Internet use can be classified as a
true addiction.

(A) Some experts warn that Net addiction can worsen
    depression and cause withdrawal from reality.
(B) Middle-aged women, the unemployed, and the new
    Internet users are most prone to Internet addiction.
(C) Normal users average only eight hours per week.
(D) However, even these experts can't decide whether
    "pathological Internet use" is an addiction, a disorder, or
    only a symptom of an addictive personality.
(E) No matter what, everyone agrees that more study is needed.

TEST 19 詳解

Do you compulsively surf the Web when you should be eating or sleeping? Such behavior has aroused the interest of psychologists. [1](D) However, even these experts can't decide whether "pathological Internet use" is an addiction, a disorder, or only a symptom of an addictive personality. They can only say that it is a new and fascinating field waiting to be explored.

當你應該吃飯或睡覺時，你會強迫性地上網嗎？這種行為已經引起心理學家們的興趣。然而，即使是這些專家，都無法決定「病態的網路使用」是一種上癮行為，一種行為失常，或者只是一種容易上癮的人格症狀。他們只能說，這是一個全新且吸引人的領域，有待人們去探索。

compulsively〔kəm'pʌlsɪvlɪ〕*adv.* 強迫性地   surf〔sɜf〕*v.* 瀏覽
the Web 網路 (= *the Net* = *the Internet*)   *surf the Web* 上網
behavior〔bɪ'hevjɚ〕*n.* 行為   arouse〔ə'raʊz〕*v.* 喚起
psychologist〔saɪ'kɑlədʒɪst〕*n.* 心理學家
expert〔'ɛkspɜt〕*n.* 專家   pathological〔ˌpæθə'lɑdʒɪkl̩〕*adj.* 不健康的
Internet〔'ɪntɚˌnɛt〕*n.* 網際網路   addiction〔ə'dɪkʃən〕*n.* 上癮
disorder〔dɪs'ɔrdɚ〕*n.* 失調；失常   symptom〔'sɪmptəm〕*n.* 症狀
addictive〔ə'dɪktɪv〕*adj.* 上癮的   personality〔ˌpɜsn̩'ælətɪ〕*n.* 人格
fascinating〔'fæsn̩ˌetɪŋ〕*adj.* 迷人的   field〔fild〕*n.* 領域
explore〔ɪk'splor〕*v.* 探索

[2](C) Normal users average only eight hours per week. An "Internet Addict" is described as anyone who spends up to 38 hours per week on-line for non-work purposes.

正常的使用者，每個禮拜平均使用八小時。「網路上癮者」則是描述任何人，在工作目的之外，每個禮拜上網時間高達三十八小時。

normal〔'nɔrml̩〕*adj.* 正常的   average〔'ævərɪdʒ〕*v.* 平均達到
addict〔'ædɪkt〕*n.* 上癮者   describe〔dɪ'skraɪb〕*v.* 描述
up to 多達   on-line〔'ɑn'laɪn〕*adv.* 上線地
non-work〔'nɑn'wɜk〕*adj.* 非工作性質的   purpose〔'pɜpəs〕*n.* 目的

³(B) Middle-aged women, the unemployed, and the new Internet users are most prone to Internet addiction. Students may also be at risk. One third of students know someone with social or academic problems which are traceable to heavy Net use. 中年婦女、失業的人、以及網路新手，最容易對網路上癮。學生可能也是危險群。三分之一的學生認識一些在社交上或學業上有問題的人，其問題都可追溯到大量使用網路。

> middle-aged〔ˈmɪdl̩ˈedʒd〕*adj.* 中年的
> unemployed〔ˌʌnɪmˈplɔɪd〕*adj.* 失業的　　***the unemployed*** 失業者
> prone〔pron〕*adj.* 有～傾向的　　***be prone to*** 容易　***at risk*** 有危險
> social〔ˈsoʃəl〕*adj.* 社交的　　academic〔ˌækəˈdɛmɪk〕*adj.* 學業的
> traceable〔ˈtresəbl̩〕*adj.* 可追溯的
> heavy〔ˈhɛvɪ〕*adj.* 常常的；大量的

⁴(A) Some experts warn that Net addiction can worsen depression and cause withdrawal from reality. Others see the Net as something that drives human beings to overdo. ⁵(E) No matter what, everyone agrees that more study is needed. We need more comprehensive research before pathological Internet use can be classified as a true addiction. 有一些專家警告，網路上癮會使憂鬱症惡化，以及導致逃避現實。其他專家則認為，網路會使人類不知節制。無論如何，每個人都同意我們需要做更多的研究。我們做更廣泛的研究之後，再來決定病態網路使用，可否被歸類成真正的上癮行為。

> warn〔wɔrn〕*v.* 警告　　net〔nɛt〕*n.* 網路
> worsen〔ˈwɝsn̩〕*v.* 惡化　　depression〔dɪˈprɛʃən〕*n.* 沮喪；憂鬱症
> cause〔kɔz〕*v.* 導致；造成　　withdrawal〔wɪðˈdrɔəl〕*n.* 退縮
> reality〔rɪˈælətɪ〕*n.* 現實　　***see A as B*** 視 A 為 B
> drive〔draɪv〕*v.* 驅使　　***human being*** 人類
> overdo〔ˈovɚˈdu〕*v.* 做得太過度；不知節制
> ***no matter what*** 無論如何　　agree〔əˈgri〕*v.* 同意
> study〔ˈstʌdɪ〕*n.* 研究　　comprehensive〔ˌkɑmprɪˈhɛnsɪv〕*adj.* 廣泛的
> research〔ˈrisɝtʃ〕*n.* 研究　　classify〔ˈklæsəˌfaɪ〕*v.* 歸類
> true〔tru〕*adj.* 真實的；真正的

TEST 20

說明： 第 1 至 5 題，每題一個空格。請依文意在文章後所提供的 (A) 到 (E) 選項中分別選出最適當者。

      __1__ or they can be man-made devices orbiting around the earth, the moon or some other planet. __2__.

      Satellites affect us all. Man-made satellites can be used to transmit scientific information to earth, they can be used for communication and they can provide an overall picture of our world. __3__ They're vital to today's world.

      Did you know that there are hundreds of artificial satellites orbiting above you as you read this? __4__ They are too faint to be seen during the day but can be seen at night provided they are still in sunlight. The best time to spot a satellite is in the early evening or before dawn.

Satellites do not give off light of their own but they reflect sunlight just as the moon does.

___5___ Bright city lights don't help much so if you can get away from cities and towns, your chances of spotting a satellite are greatly improved.

(A) Satellites can be natural bodies which orbit around a planet or star

(B) They appear as small lights moving steadily across the sky though you may need some patience to spot one.

(C) The moon is a satellite of the earth and the earth is a satellite of the sun.

(D) You can actually see many of the large ones.

(E) Information from satellites can help us to predict tomorrow's weather or next season's food crop.

TEST 20 詳解

[1](A) Satellites can be natural bodies which orbit around a planet or star or they can be man-made devices orbiting around the earth, the moon or some other planet. [2](C) The moon is a satellite of the earth and the earth is a satellite of the sun.

衛星可以是繞著行星或星體運轉的自然物體，或是繞著地球、月球或其它行星旋轉的人造裝置。月球是地球的衛星，地球是太陽的衛星。

> satellite ('sætl͵aɪt) n. 衛星　　natural ('nætʃərəl) adj. 自然的
> body ('badɪ) n. 物體　　orbit ('ɔrbɪt) v. 運轉
> planet ('plænɪt) n. 行星　　man-made ('mæn'med) adj. 人造的
> device (dɪ'vaɪs) n. 發明的東西；裝置

Satellites affect us all. Man-made satellites can be used to transmit scientific information to earth, they can be used for communication and they can provide an overall picture of our world. [3](E) Information from satellites can help us to predict tomorrow's weather or next season's food crop. They're vital to today's world.

衛星對全人類影響很大。人造衛星可用來傳送科學訊息到地球，可用來通訊，還可提供整個地球的照片。從衛星得到的資訊，可以幫助我們預測明天的天氣，或是下一季的食物產量。它們對今日的世界極為重要。

> affect (ə'fɛkt) v. 影響　　***man-made satellite*** 人造衛星
> transmit (træns'mɪt) v. 傳送　　scientific (͵saɪən'tɪfɪk) adj. 科學的
> communication (kə͵mjunə'keʃən) n. 通訊
> provide (prə'vaɪd) v. 提供　　overall ('ovɚ͵ɔl) adj. 整體的
> predict (prɪ'dɪkt) v. 預測　　crop (krap) n. 產量
> vital ('vaɪtl̩) adj. 極為重要的

Did you know that there are hundreds of artificial satellites orbiting above you as you read this? [4](**D**) <u>You can actually see many of the large ones.</u> They are too faint to be seen during the day but can be seen at night provided they are still in sunlight. The best time to spot a satellite is in the early evening or before dawn. Satellites do not give off light of their own but they reflect sunlight just as the moon does.

你知道嗎？當你閱讀這篇文章時，有數百個人造衛星在你的頭頂上運行。事實上，你可以看到許多大型衛星。白天它們的光線太微弱，很難看到，傍晚時，如果還有日光，就可以看見它們。觀看衛星最好的時間是在傍晚，或黎明前。衛星不會自己發光，但它們會反射日光，就像月球一樣。

artificial (ˌɑrtəˈfɪʃəl) *adj.* 人造的
faint (fent) *adj.* (光、聲音) 微弱的
provided (prəˈvaɪdɪd) *conj.* 倘若；如果 (= *if*)
sunlight (ˈsʌnˌlaɪt) *n.* 日光　　spot (spɑt) *v.* 發現；看出
dawn (dɔn) *n.* 黎明　　***give off*** 發出 (光、聲音)
reflect (rɪˈflɛkt) *v.* 反射

[5](**B**) <u>They appear as small lights moving steadily across the sky though you may need some patience to spot one.</u> Bright city lights don't help much so if you can get away from cities and towns, your chances of spotting a satellite are greatly improved.

它們就像是小型的發光體，慢慢橫越天空，不過你需要有耐心，才能看到衛星。城市裡的亮光是不太可能讓你看到衛星的，所以，如果你能遠離城鎮，你看見衛星的機率會大大增加。

appear (əˈpɪr) *v.* 顯現　　light (laɪt) *n.* 發光體
steadily (ˈstɛdəlɪ) *adv.* 不斷地　　patience (ˈpeʃəns) *n.* 耐心
get away from 遠離　　improve (ɪmˈpruv) *v.* 改善；增進

TEST 21

說明：第 1 至 5 題，每題一個空格。請依文意在文章後所提供的(A)到
(E) 選項中分別選出最適當者。

The first big wave of Chinese immigration to
America came when gold was discovered in
California in 1848. The Chinese called the new land
"Mountain of Gold." ___1___ By the 1880s, American
industrialization brought changing economic realities,
resulting in an explosion of resentment toward the
Chinese laborer. He was accused of taking jobs
away from the white man. ___2___ Many workers
fled from the concentrated Chinese communities in
the West and scattered to the Midwest and the East.
___3___

New York's Chinatown was created by men such
as these. Sociologists call them "sojourners" —
foreigners in the United States, clinging to their
cultural traditions, living in isolation and resisting
being absorbed into the larger society in which they

existed. ___4___ Those who did stay lived

separately from the society — the Exclusion Acts

did not allow laborers to bring their wives to

America. ___5___

(A) The sojourner came to America for the

promise of supporting his family in China,

where he expected to return one day.

(B) The government issued Exclusion Acts to

stop the immigration of Chinese laborers

into the United States.

(C) As in California, they formed small

pockets of Chinese culture that were

known as "Chinatowns."

(D) Those who did not become miners found

work in railroad construction and light

industries, doing low paid jobs.

(E) So they remained in Chinatown, an

enclosed community holding on to

traditions among the tides of change.

TEST 21 詳解

The first big wave of Chinese immigration to America came when gold was discovered in California in 1848. The Chinese called the new land "Mountain of Gold."

西元一八四八年加州發現金礦後，中國產生第一波移民到美國的巨大移民潮。中國人稱呼這個新世界爲「金山」。

wave〔wev〕*n.* 波　　immigration〔͵ɪməˋgreʃən〕*n.* 移民
discover〔dɪˋskʌvɚ〕*v.* 發現

[1](D) <u>Those who did not become miners found work in railroad construction and light industries, doing low paid jobs.</u> By the 1880s, American industrialization brought changing economic realities, resulting in an explosion of resentment toward the Chinese laborer.

那些沒有成爲礦工的人，就去參與修築鐵路，或在輕工業裡找差事做，賺取微薄的薪資。到了一八八〇年代，美國工業化的結果，帶來經濟現實面的改變，引起美國人對中國勞工急遽不滿。

miner〔ˋmaɪnɚ〕*n.* 礦工　　railroad〔ˋrel͵rod〕*n.* 鐵路
construction〔kənˋstrʌkʃən〕*n.* 修築　　***light industry*** 輕工業
industrialization〔ɪn͵dʌstrɪələˋzeʃən〕*n.* 工業化
economic〔͵ikəˋnɑmɪk〕*adj.* 經濟的
reality〔rɪˋælətɪ〕*n.* 現實　　***result in*** 導致
explosion〔ɪkˋsploʒən〕*n.* 爆發
resentment〔rɪˋzɛntmənt〕*n.* 憤怒　　laborer〔ˋlebərɚ〕*n.* 勞工

He was accused of taking jobs away from the white man. [2](B) <u>The government issued Exclusion Acts to stop the immigration of Chinese laborers into the United States.</u>

他們被指責搶了白人的工作。於是美國政府頒布了排外法案,企圖阻止中國勞工移民到美國。

> accuse〔ə'kjuz〕*v.* 譴責;控訴
> **be accused of** 被譴責　　government〔'gʌvənmənt〕*n.* 政府
> issue〔'ɪʃju〕*v.* 頒布　　exclusion〔ɪk'skluʒən〕*n.* 排除
> act〔ækt〕*n.* 法令　　**Exclusion Acts** 排外法案

Many workers fled from the concentrated Chinese communities in the West and scattered to the Midwest and the East. [3](C) As in California, they formed small pockets of Chinese culture that were known as "Chinatowns."

許多中國勞工離開西岸中國人聚集的社區,分散到中西部和東岸。正如在加州所見的,他們形成許多小型的中國文化區,這就是眾所皆知的「中國城」。

> flee〔fli〕*v.* 逃離
> concentrated〔'kɑnsn̩,tretɪd〕*adj.* 集中的
> community〔kə'mjunətɪ〕*n.* 社區
> **the west** 美國西部各州　　scatter〔'skætə〕*v.* 分散
> **the Midwest** (美國)中西部　　form〔fɔrm〕*v.* 形成
> pocket〔'pɑkɪt〕*n.* (孤立的)小地區　　**be known as** 以~著稱
> Chinatown〔'tʃaɪnə,taun〕*n.* 中國城;唐人街

New York's Chinatown was created by men such as these. Sociologists call them "sojourners" — foreigners in the United States, clinging to their cultural traditions, living in isolation and resisting being absorbed into the larger society in which they existed.

紐約的中國城，也由這些人所創建的。社會學家稱這些中國人為「寄居者」——留滯美國的外國人，固守他們的傳統文化，過著孤立的生活，不願意融入他們所處的大型社會。

> create〔krɪ'et〕v. 創造；創建
> sociologist〔ˌsoʃɪ'alədʒɪst〕n. 社會學家
> sojourner〔'sodʒʒnɚ〕n. 寄居者　　cling〔klɪŋ〕v. 執著於
> **cling to** 執著於；固守　　tradition〔trə'dɪʃən〕n. 傳統
> isolation〔ˌaɪsl'eʃən〕n. 孤立
> resist〔rɪ'zɪst〕v. 抗拒　　absorb〔əb'sɔrb〕v. 吸收；同化
> exist〔ɪg'zɪst〕v. 存在

[4](A) The sojourner came to America for the promise of supporting his family in China, where he expected to return one day. Those who did stay lived separately from the society — the Exclusion Acts did not allow laborers to bring their wives to America.

這些寄居者來到美國，都是為了養活留在中國的親人，他們也冀望有一天能夠回到家鄉。而那些回不去而留下來的人，就過著與社會脫節的生活——排外法案並不允許這些勞工帶著妻子到美國。

> promise〔'pramɪs〕n. 希望　　support〔sə'port〕v. 扶養
> expect〔ɪk'spɛkt〕v. 期望
> separately〔'sɛpəˌretlɪ〕adv. 分開地

[5](E) So they remained in Chinatown, an enclosed community holding on to traditions among the tides of change.

所以他們就留在中國城，那裡是一個封閉的社區，即使在改變的浪潮中，仍固守傳統的地方。

> remain〔rɪ'men〕v. 停留　　enclosed〔ɪn'klozd〕adj. 封閉的
> **hold on to** 繼續下去　　tide〔taɪd〕n. 潮流

TEST 22

說明：第 1 至 5 題，每題一個空格。請依文意在文章後所提供的 (A) 到 (E) 選項中分別選出最適當者。

A lot of today's pop music is too commercialized. The reason is obvious: decisions made about the music are made by the recording company and not the singers or musicians themselves.

___1___ This in itself is not a bad way of producing music. ___2___ When we watch music programs on TV or listen to them on the radio, it is often possible to tell the difference between songs that have been created in this way and those composed and performed by a singer/songwriter. ___3___ These qualities attract the listeners and, in some cases, such music has lasting value.

___4___ I firmly believe that music is one of the pleasures of life. ___5___ They should not be confined to or bombarded by the same kind of commercialized songs and music.

(A) Unfortunately, commercialized pop music is more successful nowadays.

(B) But it tends to result in songs which conform to a certain pattern and lack originality.

(C) Pop music produced by a singer/songwriter usually has something fresh and different about it.

(D) Young people, in particular, should be given the opportunity to enjoy a wide variety of music.

(E) Of course, the recording companies' main concern is to create a popular sound that will get listed on the Billboard Top 100 and make money.

TEST 22 詳解

A lot of today's pop music is too commercialized. The reason is obvious: decisions made about the music are made by the recording company and not the singers or musicians themselves.

今天有很多流行音樂都太過商業化。其原因很明顯：有關音樂的決定，都取決於唱片公司，而不是歌手或音樂家本身。

> ***pop music*** 流行音樂 (= *popular music*)
> commercialized (kə'mɝʃəl͵aɪzd) *adj.* 商業化的
> reason ('rizn̩) *n.* 理由　　obvious ('ɑbvɪəs) *adj.* 明顯的
> ***recording company*** 唱片公司　　musician (mju'zɪʃən) *n.* 音樂家

[1](E) Of course, the recording companies' main concern is to create a popular sound that will get listed on the Billboard Top 100 and make money. This in itself is not a bad way of producing music. [2](B) But it tends to result in songs which conform to a certain pattern and lack originality. When we watch music programs on TV or listen to them on the radio, it is often possible to tell the difference between songs that have been created in this way and those composed and performed by a singer/songwriter. [3](C) Pop music produced by a singer/songwriter usually has something fresh and different about it. These qualities attract the listeners and, in some cases, such music has lasting value.

當然，唱片公司最關心的事情，還是創造出受歡迎的聲音，這個聲音要可以擠入排行榜的前一百名，然後賺錢。這樣的作音樂方式，本身並不壞。但是，這很容易導致歌曲流於某種形式，或是缺乏創意。當我們收看電視，或收聽廣播的音樂節目時，常常可以區分出這些歌曲是用這種方式創作，或由歌手/作曲人所創作以及演奏的。歌手/作曲人所創作的流行音

樂，通常會比較清新及不同。這些特質很吸引聽衆，在某些例子當中，這
種音樂甚至有永恆的價值。

> main〔men〕*adj.* 主要的　　concern〔kən'sɜn〕*n.* 關心的事
> create〔krɪ'et〕*v.* 創作；創造　　list〔lɪst〕*v.* 列於表中
> billboard〔'bɪl,bord〕*n.* 排行榜；告示榜
> produce〔prə'djus〕*v.* 製作　　tend〔tɛnd〕*v.* 傾向 < *to* >
> *result in* 導致　　conform〔kən'fɔrm〕*v.* 和～一致< *to* >
> certain〔'sɜtn̩〕*adj.* 某一種的　　pattern〔'pætən〕*n.* 形式
> lack〔læk〕*v.* 缺乏　　originality〔ə,rɪdʒə'næləti〕*n.* 創意
> tell〔tɛl〕*v.* 分辨　　compose〔kəm'poz〕*v.* 作曲
> perform〔pɚ'fɔrm〕*v.* 演奏
> songwriter〔'sɔŋ,raɪtɚ〕*n.* 作曲家　　fresh〔frɛʃ〕*adj.* 清新的
> quality〔'kwɑləti〕*n.* 特質　　case〔kes〕*n.* 例子；情況
> lasting〔'læstɪŋ〕*adj.* 持久的；永恆的　　value〔'vælju〕*n.* 價值

[4](A) Unfortunately, commercialized pop music is more successful
nowadays. I firmly believe that music is one of the pleasures of life.
[5](D) Young people, in particular, should be given the opportunity to
enjoy a wide variety of music. They should not be confined to or
bombarded by the same kind of commercialized songs and music.
不幸的是，現今商業化的流行音樂比較受歡迎。我堅信，音樂是生活的樂
趣之一。特別是年輕人，應該要有多一點機會，去享受各式各樣不同的音
樂。他們不應該受限於同一種商業化的歌曲或音樂，或被這樣的音樂疲勞
轟炸。

> unfortunately〔ʌn'fɔrtʃənɪtlɪ〕*adv.* 不幸地
> firmly〔'fɜmlɪ〕*adv.* 堅定地　　pleasure〔'plɛʒɚ〕*n.* 樂趣
> *in particular* 特別是　　opportunity〔,ɑpɚ'tjunətɪ〕*n.* 機會
> *a variety of* 各式各樣的（ = *various* ）
> confine〔kən'faɪn〕*v.* 限制
> bombard〔bɑm'bɑrd〕*v.*（疲勞）轟炸

TEST 23

Thousands of Americans notice friends or daughters going beyond skinny to skeletal, and the urge to confront loved ones showing signs of anorexia —— "Will you please just eat?!" —— can be powerful.

But mental health professionals counsel gentle persuasion over hard lobbying. Friends and family need to realize ___1___

"You want to avoid getting into a full frontal assault because that almost always ends badly," said Dr. Doug Bunnell, a clinical psychologist.

Anorexia nervosa is a psychological disorder ___2___ Some exercise obsessively ; others use laxatives or force themselves to vomit.

An excruciating feature of the disorder is that it can seem to unfold in slow motion in front of friends and family as the sufferer gets progressively thinner. ___3___ Should I say anything? What do I say? When?

The eating disorders association cautions people not to worsen the situation with admonitions like "You just need to eat!" or "You are acting irresponsibly." ___4___

"One of the hallmarks of the illness is denial of the illness," Bunnell said. "So if you go at someone really harshly or in a confrontational way, you're just going to evoke a real defensive reaction."

An intervention does not always work the first time. ___5___ All they can do, he said, is keep speaking honestly about their concerns. 【北模】

(A) Loved ones are typically tormented by the same questions:

(B) Hard as it may be to do so, Bunnell said, friends and family have to accept that they are powerless.

(C) Try a softer tack, with phrases like "I'm concerned about you." Be supportive.

(D) that an anorexic looking in the mirror does not see the same emaciated figure they do.

(E) in which the sufferer becomes exceedingly thin and still believes he or she is overweight.

TEST 23 詳解

Thousands of Americans notice friends or daughters going beyond skinny to skeletal, and the urge to confront loved ones showing signs of anorexia — "Will you please just eat?!" — can be powerful.

　　數千名美國人發覺朋友或女兒，已經超過很瘦的範圍，而到達骨瘦如柴的程度了，這些人可能會有很強烈的衝動，想當面告訴所愛的人——「能不能拜託你吃點東西?!」——因為他們已經出現厭食症的症狀了。

> ***thousands of*** 數以千計的　　notice ('notɪs) v. 發覺；注意到
> ***go beyond*** 超過　　skinny ('skɪnɪ) adj. 很瘦的；皮包骨的
> skeletal ('skɛlətəl) adj. 骨瘦如柴的
> urge (ɝdʒ) n. 衝動　　confront (kən'frʌnt) v. 與…面對面
> loved (lʌvd) adj. 親愛的；珍愛的　　***loved ones*** 親愛的人；親人
> show (ʃo) v. 顯現　　sign (saɪn) n. 徵兆；症狀
> anorexia (ˏænə'rɛksɪə) n. 厭食
> powerful ('pauɚfəl) adj. 強烈的

But mental health professionals counsel gentle persuasion over hard lobbying. Friends and family need to realize ¹**(D) that an anorexic looking in the mirror does not see the same emaciated figure they do.**

　　但是心理健康方面的專家建議，柔性勸說勝於拼命的遊說。朋友和家人必須了解，厭食者從鏡子裡看到的，和他們所看到的削瘦身材是不同的。

> mental ('mɛntl̩) adj. 心理的
> professional (prə'fɛʃənl̩) n. 專家
> counsel ('kaunsl̩) v. 建議　　gentle ('dʒɛntl̩) adj. 溫柔的
> persuasion (pɚ'sweʒən) n. 勸說　　over ('ovɚ) prep. 勝過
> hard (hard) adj. 拼命的；猛烈的　　lobbying ('labɪɪŋ) n. 遊說

anorexic〔͵ænəˈrɛksɪk〕*n.* 厭食者　　mirror〔ˈmɪrə〕*n.* 鏡子
same〔sem〕*adj.* 相同的　　emaciated〔ɪˈmeʃɪ͵etɪd〕*adj.* 削瘦的
figure〔ˈfɪgjə〕*n.* 身材

"You want to avoid getting into a full frontal assault because that almost always ends badly," said Dr. Doug Bunnell, a clinical psychologist.

　「你要避免陷入完全的正面攻擊，因爲那幾乎總是會帶來不好的結果，」臨床心理學家道格・班尼爾博士說。

get into 進入；陷入　　frontal〔ˈfrʌntl̩〕*adj.* 正面的
assault〔əˈsɔlt〕*n.* 攻擊　　end〔ɛnd〕*v.* 結束
clinical〔ˈklɪnɪkl̩〕*adj.* 臨床的
psychologist〔saɪˈkɑlədʒɪst〕*n.* 心理學家

Anorexia nervosa is a psychological disorder [2](E) in which the sufferer becomes exceedingly thin and still believes he or she is overweight. Some exercise obsessively; others use laxatives or force themselves to vomit.

　神經性厭食症是一種心理疾病，罹患這種疾病的人，會變得非常瘦，但卻還認爲自己超重。有些人會過度運動；有些人則是服用瀉藥，或強迫自己嘔吐。

anorexia nervosa 精神性厭食症
psychological〔͵saɪkəˈlɑdʒɪkl̩〕*adj.* 心理上的
disorder〔dɪsˈɔrdə〕*n.* 失調；疾病　　sufferer〔ˈsʌfərə〕*n.* 患者
exceedingly〔ɪkˈsidɪŋlɪ〕*adv.* 非常地　　thin〔θɪn〕*adj.* 瘦的
overweight〔ˈovəˈwet〕*adj.* 超重的
exercise〔ˈɛksə͵saɪz〕*v.* 運動
obsessively〔əbˈsɛsɪvlɪ〕*adv.* 過度地
laxative〔ˈlæksətɪv〕*n.* 瀉藥
force〔fors〕*v.* 強迫　　vomit〔ˈvɑmɪt〕*v.* 嘔吐

An excruciating feature of the disorder is that it can seem to unfold in slow motion in front of friends and family as the sufferer gets progressively thinner.

這種疾病最令人難以忍受的特色，就是它似乎是以慢動作的方式，慢慢呈現在朋友和家人面前，也就是患者會變得愈來愈瘦。

excruciating (ɪkˋskruʃɪˏetɪŋ) *adj.* 折磨人的；令人難以忍受的
feature (ˋfitʃɚ) *n.* 特色　　unfold (ʌnˋfold) *v.* 展現；呈現
motion (ˋmoʃən) *n.* 動作　　*in slow motion* 以慢動作
in front of 在～面前
progressively (prəˋgrɛsɪvlɪ) *adv.* 逐漸地；愈來愈嚴重地

3(A) Loved ones are typically tormented by the same questions: Should I say anything? What do I say? When?

親人經常會被相同的問題所折磨：我應該說什麼嗎？我該說什麼？什麼時候說才好？

typically (ˋtɪpɪk!ɪ) *adv.* 經常　　torment (tɔrˋmɛnt) *v.* 折磨

The eating disorders association cautions people not to worsen the situation with admonitions like "You just need to eat!" or "You are acting irresponsibly." 4(C) Try a softer tack, with phrases like "I'm concerned about you." Be supportive.

飲食失調協會提醒我們，不要用會讓情況更糟的勸告方式，像是「你就是得吃！」或「你這樣的行為很不負責任。」試試看比較溫和的方式，用像是「我很關心你。」這樣的說法。要和藹地對待他們。

association (əˏsoʃɪˋeʃən) *n.* 協會
caution (ˋkɔʃən) *v.* 警告；提醒
worsen (ˋwɝsn̩) *v.* 使更壞；使惡化
situation (ˏsɪtʃʊˋeʃən) *n.* 情況
admonition (ˏædməˋnɪʃən) *n.* 勸告　　act (ækt) *v.* 行為；表現
irresponsibly (ˏɪrɪˋspɑnsəblɪ) *adv.* 不負責任地

tack ﹝ tæk ﹞ *n.* 方針；政策；社交手腕　　phrase ﹝ frez ﹞ *n.* 說法
concerned ﹝ kən'sɜnd ﹞ *adj.* 關心的
supportive ﹝ sə'pɔrtɪv ﹞ *adj.* 支持的；和藹地對待的

"One of the hallmarks of the illness is denial of the illness,"
Bunnell said. "So if you go at someone really harshly or in a
confrontational way, you're just going to evoke a real defensive
reaction."

　　「這種疾病的特色之一，就是會否認患病，」班尼爾說。「所以如
果你用真的很嚴厲或是對立的方式，來打擊某個人，那麼你只會引起
真正的自衛反應。」

hallmark ﹝'hɔl,mɑrk ﹞ *n.* 特色　　illness ﹝'ɪlnɪs ﹞ *n.* 疾病
denial ﹝ dɪ'naɪəl ﹞ *n.* 否認　　***go at*** （以嚴厲的口氣）攻擊；打擊
harshly ﹝'hɑrʃlɪ ﹞ *adv.* 嚴厲地
confrontational ﹝,kɑnfrən'teʃənl ﹞ *adj.* 對立的
evoke ﹝ ɪ'vok ﹞ *v.* 引起
defensive ﹝ dɪ'fɛnsɪv ﹞ *adj.* 自衛的；保衛的
reaction ﹝ rɪ'ækʃən ﹞ *n.* 反應

An intervention does not always work the first time. [5](B) Hard
as it may be to do so, Bunnell said, friends and family have to
accept that they are powerless. All they can do, he said, is keep
speaking honestly about their concerns.

　　第一次干涉時，不一定有用。班尼爾說，雖然這麼做很困難，但是
朋友和家人必須接受自己是無能為力的。他說，他們所能做的，就是不
斷地誠實說出自己的關心。

intervention ﹝,ɪntɚ'vɛnʃən ﹞ *n.* 介入；干涉
work ﹝ wɜk ﹞ *v.* 有效；行得通
Hard as it may be … 「雖然…可能很困難」，句中的 as 作「雖然」解。
powerless ﹝'paʊɚlɪs ﹞ *adj.* 無能為力的
All one can do is V. 某人所能做的，就是～
honestly ﹝'ɑnɪstlɪ ﹞ *adv.* 誠實地　　concern ﹝ kən'sɜn ﹞ *n.* 關心

TEST 24

說明： 第 1 至 5 題，每題一個空格。請依文意在文章後所提供的 (A) 到 (E) 選項中分別選出最適當者。

Online transactions have gradually become accepted among consumers in Taiwan. ___1___ The amount of money exchanged in this manner was generally small per transaction. Nevertheless, the value of online purchases has dramatically increased every year for the past three years.

___2___ For example, baby items and formula companies have successfully sold their bulky products via the Internet. Their Internet sales service has proven popular among pregnant women and new mothers because of the convenient home delivery. ___3___ Many of them offer free delivery by allowing customers to pick up their ordered books at a convenient location in their neighborhood.

Furthermore, the Internet allows sellers to efficiently manage the supply of goods. ___4___ With pre-orders, consumers can receive the latest issue of a magazine before other people do. Suppliers can adjust their inventory without piling on excessive stock. Retailers can also sell old items over the Internet.

   5   Consumers can therefore count on service providers for more new ideas. 【94 研究試卷】

(A) For certain items, the Internet provides a promising channel.

(B) Many suppliers have found that pre-orders have worked well online.

(C) In 2002, sales generated by e-commerce in Taiwan were a mere 0.5 percent of total retail sales islandwide.

(D) It is certain that e-commerce will continue to grow in the Taiwan market.

(E) Online book sellers have also increased their sales due to fast delivery of orders.

TEST 24 詳解

Online transactions have gradually become accepted among consumers in Taiwan. [1](C) In 2002, sales generated by e-commerce in Taiwan were a mere 0.5 percent of total retail sales islandwide.

線上交易已經逐漸被台灣的消費者所接受了。二○○二年時,台灣經由電子交易所產生的銷售額,只佔了全島各地零售銷售總額的百分之零點五。

online ('ɑn,laɪn) *adj.* 線上的;網路的
transaction (træns'ækʃən) *n.* 交易;買賣
gradually ('grædʒʊəlɪ) *adv.* 逐漸地   sales (selz) *n. pl.* 銷售額
generate ('dʒɛnə,ret) *v.* 產生   *e-commerce* *n.* 電子交易
mere (mɪr) *adj.* 僅僅;只是   percent (pə'sɛnt) *n.* 百分之…
retail ('ritel) *adj.* 零售的   islandwide ('aɪlənd'waɪd) *adv.* 全島各地

The amount of money exchanged in this manner was generally small per transaction. Nevertheless, the value of online purchases has dramatically increased every year for the past three years.

以這種方式交易的每一筆交易金額,通常都很小。儘管如此,在過去三年來,網路購物的金額,每年都大幅地增加。

exchange (ɪks'tʃendʒ) *v.* 交易;交換
generally ('dʒɛnərəlɪ) *adv.* 通常   value ('vælju) *n.* 價值;價格
dramatically (drə'mætɪklɪ) *adv.* 顯著地;相當地

[2](A) For certain items, the Internet provides a promising channel. For example, baby items and formula companies have successfully sold their bulky products via the Internet.

就某些物品而言,網路提供了比較有希望的管道。例如,嬰兒用品與嬰兒奶粉公司,已成功地透過網路來銷售他們的大型產品。

certain ('sɝtn) *adj.* 某些
promising ('prɑmɪsɪŋ) *adj.* 有希望的;有可能的
channel ('tʃænl) *n.* 管道;途徑   formula ('fɔrmjələ) *n.* 嬰兒奶粉
bulky ('bʌlkɪ) *adj.* 大型的;不易處理的   via ('vaɪə) *prep.* 經由

Their Internet sales service has proven popular among pregnant women and new mothers because of the convenient home delivery. ³(E) Online book sellers have also increased their sales due to fast delivery of orders. Many of them offer free delivery by allowing customers to pick up their ordered books at a convenient location in their neighborhood. 因爲有方便的宅配,所以他們的網路銷售服務,很受孕婦和剛當母親的人歡迎。網路書店的銷售額,也由於能快速交貨而增加。他們很多都提供免運費的服務,讓顧客到鄰近地區的方便地點,去拿他們訂的書。

pregnant ('prɛgnənt) adj. 懷孕的　　delivery (dɪ'lɪvərɪ) n. 遞送
home delivery 宅配;送貨到府　　order ('ɔrdə) n. 訂單;訂貨
pick up 拿走　　ordered ('ɔrdəd) adj. 訂購的

Furthermore, the Internet allows sellers to efficiently manage the supply of goods. ⁴(B) Many suppliers have found that pre-orders have worked well online. With pre-orders, consumers can receive the latest issue of a magazine before other people do. Suppliers can adjust their inventory without piling on excessive stock. Retailers can also sell old items over the Internet. 此外,網路讓賣家可以有效率地管理商品的供應。許多賣家發現,上網預訂的效果不錯。有預訂的顧客,可以比其他人早一步收到最新一期的雜誌。賣家能調節庫存,而不用堆積過多的存貨。零售商也可以透過網路,來賣掉舊貨。

efficiently (ə'fɪʃəntlɪ) adv. 有效率地　　manage ('mænɪdʒ) v. 管理
pre-order (pri'ɔrdə) n. 預訂　　issue ('ɪʃju) n. (雜誌的) 期
inventory ('ɪnvən,torɪ) n. 存貨;庫存　　pile (paɪl) v. 堆積
excessive (ɪk'sɛsɪv) adj. 過多的　　retailer ('ritelə) n. 零售商

⁵(D) It is certain that e-commerce will continue to grow in the Taiwan market. Consumers can therefore count on service providers for more new ideas. 可以確定的是,電子交易將在台灣的市場中繼續成長。因此,消費者也可以仰賴提供服務的人,來提供更多的新構想。

certain ('sɜtn̩) adj. 確定的　　**count on** 仰賴;指望

TEST 25

說明： 第 1 至 5 題，每題一個空格。請依文意在文章後所提供的 (A) 到 (E) 選項中分別選出最適當者。

CPR stands for cardiopulmonary resuscitation. Cardio is a medical word for heart, pulmonary refers to lungs, and resuscitate means to bring back to life.

___1___ It is an amazing idea that there is a cure for sudden death. It is equally amazing this magic is not done by today's high technology. ___2___ When you give CPR, you breathe directly into the patient's mouth and start his lungs working; then, you press on the heart with your hands to make it start beating again. ___3___ It is as easy as that.

There are three common situations when CPR can be used. ___4___ One of the symptoms of a heart attack is a feeling of pressure and tightness or aching in the center of the chest. The person having a heart attack may also start sweating, feel weak, be short of breath, and feel like vomiting.

Electric shock is another situation where CPR can be applied. An electric shock usually happens to someone who has been working carelessly with electricity.   __5__   A third situation is drowning, which happens most often in the summer when many people go swimming. Children can also drown when they are left alone near a swimming pool. A person trained in CPR can help a person start to breathe after clearing the water out of the airway.

【彰化高中複習考】

(A) It can also be caused if lightning strikes a
    person.

(B) It can be used when a person has a heart
    attack and the heart stops.

(C) You continue alternating these two actions.

(D) CPR starts someone's lungs and heart
    functioning
    again after they have stopped.

(E) Any ordinary person who has learned it can
    do it.

TEST 25 詳解

CPR stands for cardiopulmonary resuscitation. Cardio is a medical word for heart, pulmonary refers to lungs, and resuscitate means to bring back to life.

CPR 代表心肺復甦術。Cardio 是心臟的醫學用語，pulmonary 指的是肺，而 resuscitate 的意思是復活。

> **CPR** 心肺復甦術 (為 cardiopulmonary resuscitation 的縮寫)
> **stand for** 代表
> cardiopulmonary resuscitation〔͵kɑrdɪə'pʌlmə͵nɛrɪ rɪ͵sʌsə'teʃən〕
>   *n.* 心肺復甦術
> **cardio-** 是表示「心臟」的字首
> for〔fɔr〕*prep.* 代表；意思是
> pulmonary〔'pʌlmə͵nɛrɪ〕*adj.* 肺的
> lung〔lʌŋ〕*n.* 肺   resuscitate〔rɪ'sʌsə͵tet〕*v.* 復甦
> **bring back to life** 使復活

[1](**D**) CPR starts someone's lungs and heart functioning again after they have stopped. It is an amazing idea that there is a cure for sudden death.

心肺復甦術可以使已經停止運作的肺和心臟，又開始運作。令人驚訝的是，居然有能醫治猝死的方法。

> function〔'fʌŋkʃən〕*v.* 運作   cure〔kjʊr〕*n.* 治療法
> sudden〔'sʌdn̩〕*adj.* 突然的   **sudden death** 猝死

It is equally amazing this magic is not done by today's high
technology. ²(E) Any ordinary person who has learned it can do it.
同樣令人驚訝的是，這並不是現代高科技所變出來的魔術。任何一個
學過心肺復甦術的普通人，都可以辦到。

> ordinary (ˈɔrdnˌɛrɪ) *adj.* 普通的；平凡的

When you give CPR, you breathe directly into the patient's mouth
and start his lungs working; then, you press on the heart with your
hands to make it start beating again.
當你施行心肺復甦術時，你要直接吹氣到患者的口中，使他的肺開始
運作；然後，你要用雙手去壓心臟，使它再度開始跳動。

> breathe (brið) *v.* 呼吸；呼出
> patient (ˈpeʃənt) *n.* 病人
> work (wɜk) *v.* 運作　　beat (bit) *v.* 跳動

³(C) You continue alternating these two actions. It is as easy as
that. 你要不斷交替做這兩個動作。就是那麼簡單。

> alternate (ˈɔltəˌnet) *v.* 交替；輪流
> *It is as easy as that.* 就是那麼簡單。(= *It is that simple.*)

There are three common situations when CPR can be used.
⁴(B) It can be used when a person has a heart attack and the heart
stops.

常用到心肺復甦術的情況有三種。它可以被用在心臟病發作，且心臟停止跳動的人身上。

> ***heart attack*** 心臟病發作
> symptom (ˋsɪmptəm) *n.* 症狀

One of the symptoms of a heart attack is a feeling of pressure and tightness or aching in the center of the chest.
心臟病發作的症狀之一，就是覺得胸中有壓迫感、胸口悶，或是會痛。

> pressure (ˋprɛʃɚ) *n.* 壓迫感
> tightness (ˋtaɪtnɪs) *n.* 緊；緊張
> aching (ˋekɪŋ) *n.* 疼痛　　chest (tʃɛst) *n.* 胸腔

The person having a heart attack may also start sweating, feel weak, be short of breath, and feel like vomiting.
心臟病發作的人，也有可能會開始流汗、感到很虛弱、呼吸急促，還有想吐。

> sweat (swɛt) *v.* 流汗　　weak (wik) *adj.* 虛弱的
> breath (brɛθ) *n.* 呼吸
> ***be short of breath*** 喘氣；呼吸急促
> ***feel like V-ing*** 想要～　　vomit (ˋvɑmɪt) *v.* 嘔吐

Electric shock is another situation where CPR can be applied. An electric shock usually happens to someone who has been working carelessly with electricity. [5](A) It can also be caused if lightning strikes a person.

　　觸電是另一個會用到心肺復甦術的情況。觸電通常發生在用電不慎的人身上。如果被閃電擊中，也有可能造成觸電。

　　electric〔ɪˈlɛktrɪk〕*adj.* 電的
　　electric shock 電擊；觸電
　　apply〔əˈplaɪ〕*v.* 施行；應用　　***work with*** 處理
　　electricity〔ɪˌlɛkˈtrɪsətɪ〕*n.* 電
　　lightning〔ˈlaɪtnɪŋ〕*n.* 閃電
　　strike〔straɪk〕*v.* 擊中

A third situation is drowning, which happens most often in the summer when many people go swimming. Children can also drown when they are left alone near a swimming pool.
第三種情況是溺水，夏天最常發生溺水，因為很多人會去游泳。當兒童被單獨留在泳池邊時，也有可能會溺水。

　　drowning〔ˈdraʊnɪŋ〕*n.* 溺水
　　drown〔draʊn〕*v.* 溺水
　　leave〔liv〕*v.* 使…維持某種狀態

A person trained in CPR can help a person start to breathe after clearing the water out of the airway.
受過心肺復甦術訓練的人，在把水清出溺水者的氣道之後，就可以幫助他開始呼吸。

　　clear A ***out of*** B　清出 B 中的 A
　　airway〔ˈɛrˌwe〕*n.*（肺的）氣道

TEST 26

說明： 第 1 至 5 題，每題一個空格。請依文意在文章後所提供的 (A) 到
(E) 選項中分別選出最適當者。

The idea that humanity was once divided into a series
of biologically distinct races which differed in quality has
had a disastrous impact. The Nazi experiments on the
Jews during World War II is probably the most tragic
example. ___1___

New technology now allows us to look at the structure
of genes in many ways. As much of modern medicine
depends on genetics, we have come to know more about
human genetic patterns than ever before. ___2___

According to recent studies, most human genes, like
skin color, blood group or alcohol tolerance, do vary from
place to place. Yet, the picture of human diversity does
not exhibit clear signs of racial differences. ___3___
Instead, the patterns of variation in blood groups, proteins
or DNA are largely independent of each other, and, more
importantly, of the patterns in the way we look.

Genetic research further shows that around 85 percent
of total human diversity comes from the differences
between individuals from the same country: two randomly

chosen Englishmen, say, or two Nigerians. Another five to 10 percent is due to the differences between nations —— for example, the people of England and Spain; of Nigeria and Kenya. The overall genetic differences between "races" —— Africans and Europeans, say —— is no greater than that between different countries within Europe or within Africa. ___4___

It may now be concluded that much of the story of the genetics of race has largely been prejudice dressed up as science. ___5___ Therefore, they make every effort to distance themselves from it. 【93 研究試卷】

(A) Most geneticists today are genuinely ashamed of the early history of their subject.

(B) The concept of race, however, is severely challenged by the latest genetic research.

(C) Variations in skin color, for example, are not accompanied by those in other genes.

(D) Hundreds of different genes have now been mapped among people across the world.

(E) Overall, the figures show that individuals —— not nations and not races —— are the main factor that accounts for human variation.

TEST 26 詳解

The idea that humanity was once divided into a series of biologically distinct races which differed in quality has had a disastrous impact.

人類曾被分成一系列不同的生物種族，而這些種族的差別，是在於品質，這樣的想法帶來了毀滅性的影響。

> humanity (hju'mænətɪ) *n.* 人類；人
> **be divided into** 被分成　　**a series of** 一系列的
> biologically (ˌbaɪə'lɑdʒɪk!ɪ) *adv.* 生物學上
> distinct (dɪ'stɪŋkt) *adj.* 不同的
> disastrous (dɪz'æstrəs) *adj.* 毀滅性的；悲慘的
> impact ('ɪmpækt) *n.* 影響

The Nazi experiments on the Jews during World War II is probably the most tragic example.

納粹在第二次世界大戰期間，對猶太人所做的實驗，可能就是最悲慘的例子。

> Nazi ('nɑtsɪ) *adj.* 納粹黨的
> experiment (ɪk'spɛrəmənt) *n.* 實驗
> Jew (dʒu) *n.* 猶太人　　tragic ('trædʒɪk) *adj.* 悲慘的

[1](B) The concept of race, however, is severely challenged by the latest genetic research.

但是種族思想在最近的基因研究中，受到了嚴厲的質疑。

concept〔'kɑnsɛpt〕*n.* 概念；思想
severely〔sə'vɪrlɪ〕*adv.* 嚴厲地
challenge〔'tʃælɪndʒ〕*n.* 質疑；挑戰
genetic〔dʒə'nɛtɪk〕*adj.* 遺傳的；基因的

New technology now allows us to look at the structure of genes in many ways. As much of modern medicine depends on genetics, we have come to know more about human genetic patterns than ever before.

現在的新科技，讓我們可以藉由很多方式，來看清楚基因的構造。而且因爲現代醫學很多都是仰賴遺傳學，所以我們也比以前更了解人類的基因型態。

> structure〔'strʌktʃ♦〕*n.* 構造
> gene〔dʒin〕*n.* 基因
> modern〔'mɑdən〕*adj.* 現代的
> genetics〔dʒə'nɛtɪks〕*n.* 遺傳學
> ***come to*** 變成　　pattern〔'pætən〕*n.* 型態
> ***than ever before*** 比以前

²**(D)** Hundreds of different genes have now been mapped among people across the world.

目前，世界各地的人，已經繪出了數百個不同的基因圖譜。

> map〔mæp〕*v.* 繪製圖譜
> ***across the world*** 全世界的

According to recent studies, most human genes, like skin color, blood group or alcohol tolerance, do vary from place to place.

根據最近的研究，人類大多數的基因，像是膚色、血型或酒量，都是因地而異的。

> ***blood group*** 血型 (= *blood type*)
> alcohol ('ælkə,hɔl) *n.* 酒
> tolerance ('tɑlərəns) *n.* 忍耐力
> ***alcohol tolerance*** 酒精耐受性；酒量
> vary ('vɛrɪ) *v.* 不同
> ***vary from place to place*** 每個地方都不同

Yet, the picture of human diversity does not exhibit clear signs of racial differences.

但是，人類的差異，並沒有明確地顯示出種族的差異。

> picture ('pɪktʃə) *n.* 狀況
> diversity (daɪ'vɜsətɪ) *n.* 差異
> exhibit (ɪg'zɪbɪt) *v.* 顯示　　　sign (saɪn) *n.* 徵兆；跡象
> racial ('reʃəl) *adj.* 種族的
> difference ('dɪfərəns) *n.* 不同；差異

[3](**C**) Variations in skin color, for example, are not accompanied by those in other genes.

舉例來說，其他基因上的差異，並不會連帶使膚色有所不同。

> variation (ˌvɛrɪ'eʃən) *n.* 差別；差異
> accompany (ə'kʌmpənɪ) *v.* 伴隨

Instead, the patterns of variation in blood groups, proteins or DNA are largely independent of each other, and, more importantly, of the patterns in the way we look.

在血型、蛋白質或去氧核醣核酸上的型態差異，彼此之間大多是毫不相關的，而且更重要的是，這些東西和我們的長相也無關。

instead (ɪnˈstɛd) adv. 取而代之
protein (ˈprotiɪn) n. 蛋白質　　**DNA** 去氧核醣核酸
largely (ˈlɑrdʒlɪ) adv. 主要地；大多
independent (ˌɪndɪˈpɛndənt) adj. 獨立的
be independent of 與…無關　　way (we) n. 樣子

Genetic research further shows that around 85 percent of total human diversity comes from the differences between individuals from the same country: two randomly chosen Englishmen, say, or two Nigerians.

基因研究更進一步顯示，全體人類的差異，有百分之八十五是來自個體間的差異，而且這些個體是來自同一個國家：比如說隨便選兩個英國人，或是兩個奈及利亞人。

further (ˈfɝðɚ) adv. 更進一步地
individual (ˌɪndəˈvɪdʒuəl) n. 個體
randomly (ˈrændəmlɪ) adv. 隨便地；胡亂地
say (se) adv. 比如說
Nigerian (naɪˈdʒɪrɪən) n. 奈及利亞人

Another five to 10 percent is due to the differences between nations —— for example, the people of England and Spain; of Nigeria and Kenya.

而另外的百分之五到十,則是因為國家的差異 —— 例如英國人和西班牙人;奈及利亞人和肯亞人。

> *due to* 由於　　nation (ˈneʃən) *n.* 國家
> England (ˈɪŋglənd) *n.* 英國
> Spain (spen) *n.* 西班牙
> Nigeria (naɪˈdʒɪrɪə) *n.* 奈及利亞
> Kenya (ˈkɛnjə) *n.* 肯亞共和國

The overall genetic differences between "races" —— Africans and Europeans, say —— is no greater than that between different countries within Europe or within Africa.

「種族」間的所有基因差異 —— 比如說非洲人和歐洲人 —— 絕對沒有比歐洲各國間的基因差異來得大,而非洲各國也同樣如此。

> overall (ˈovɚˌɔl) *adj.* 全部的;整體的
> African (ˈæfrɪkən) *n.* 非洲人
> European (ˌjurəˈpiən) *n.* 歐洲人
> no (no) *adv.* 絕不是;絕非
> within (wɪðˈɪn) *prep.* 在…之內
> Europe (ˈjurəp) *n.* 歐洲　　Africa (ˈæfrɪkə) *n.* 非洲

[4](E) Overall, the figures show that individuals —— not nations and not races —— are the main factor that accounts for human variation.

大體上,這些數字顯示,個體才是人類差異的主因,而非國家或種族。

> overall (ˌovɚˈɔl) *adv.* 大體上
> figure (ˈfɪgjɚ) *n.* 數字　　main (men) *adj.* 主要的
> factor (ˈfæktɚ) *n.* 因素　　*account for* 說明;解釋

It may now be concluded that much of the story of the genetics of race has largely been prejudice dressed up as science.

現在，我們也許可以斷定，許多關於種族遺傳的說法，主要都是由歧視所僞裝成的科學。

> conclude〔kən'klud〕*v.* 下結論；推斷
> story〔'storɪ〕*n.* 說法
> prejudice〔'prɛdʒədɪs〕*n.* 歧視
> ***dress up*** 僞裝

[5](A) Most geneticists today are genuinely ashamed of the early history of their subject.

現在，大多數的遺傳學家，都發自內心地以這個主題的早期歷史爲恥。

> geneticist〔dʒə'nɛtəsɪst〕*n.* 遺傳學家
> genuinely〔'dʒɛnjʊɪnlɪ〕*adv.* 眞地；出自內心地
> ashamed〔ə'ʃemd〕*adj.* 感到羞恥的
> ***be ashamed of*** 以～爲恥
> subject〔'sʌbdʒɪkt〕*n.*（議論、研究等的）主題；問題；題目

Therefore, they make every effort to distance themselves from it.

因此，他們都盡其所能地遠離這個主題。

> therefore〔'ðɛr‚for〕*adv.* 因此
> effort〔'ɛfət〕*n.* 努力
> ***make every effort*** 盡力
> distance〔'dɪstəns〕*v.* 使遠離

TEST 27

說明： 第 1 至 5 題，每題一個空格。請依文意在文章後所提供的 (A) 到
(E) 選項中分別選出最適當者。

Intelligence is a hot topic among educators. ___1___
Do differences in intelligence result from hereditary or
environmental influences?

On the basis of IQ scores, there is no difference
between men and women. Females do better in fine
dexterity (the ability to manipulate small objects).
___2___ This seems to indicate that some differences
are due to innate factors. But in some research papers,
educational experiences or environmental influences
seem to account for such variation. ___3___

A study has revealed that twins usually have
similar IQs even if brought up in different environments.
But according to some opposing data, environment is
supposed to affect the development of intellectual
powers. ___4___ Even scientific investigation fails to
provide a definite answer. The reason is that there is

no satisfactory definition of intelligence. Besides, we cannot cope with the limitations of research design. For example, we cannot put two people who apparently have different genes in identical environments. ___5___ Therefore, the question remains unanswered. 【中正高中期中考】

(A) Nor can we forcibly put identical twins in different environments for the research.

(B) By contrast, males get higher scores on tests of mathematical reasoning and spatial relations.

(C) So, we cannot say intelligence is genetic or environmental in origin.

(D) With no data concerning the superiority of male intelligence over the female, we had better accept the answer: "It depends."

(E) Is there any difference between men and women in measures of global IQ?

TEST 27 詳解

Intelligence is a hot topic among educators. [1](E) Is there any difference between men and women in measures of global IQ?

智力在教育家之間，是很熱門的話題。在衡量綜合智商時，男女之間有什麼差異嗎？

> intelligence〔 ɪn'tɛlədʒəns 〕 *n.* 智力；聰明
> measure〔 'mɛʒɚ 〕 *n.* 測量
> global〔 'globḷ 〕 *adj.* 綜合的
> ***IQ*** *n.* 智商（ = *intelligence quotient* ）

Do differences in intelligence result from hereditary or environmental influences?

智力的差異是因為遺傳或環境所造成的影響嗎？

> ***result from*** 起因於；由於
> hereditary〔 hə'rɛdə,tɛrɪ 〕 *adj.* 遺傳的
> environmental〔 ɪn,vaɪrən'mɛntḷ 〕 *adj.* 環境的

On the basis of IQ scores, there is no difference between men and women.

以智商分數為基礎的話，男女之間並沒有什麼差別。

> female〔 'fimel 〕 *n.* 女性
> fine〔 faɪn 〕 *adj.* 細微的

Females do better in fine dexterity (the ability to manipulate small objects).

女性在需要細微靈敏的項目上（也就是操縱小東西的能力），表現得比較好。

> dexterity (dɛks'tɛrətɪ) *n.* 靈巧；敏捷
> ability (ə'bɪlətɪ) *n.* 能力
> manipulate (mə'nɪpjə,let) *v.* 操縱

[2](**B**) By contrast, males get higher scores on tests of mathematical reasoning and spatial relations.

相較之下，男性在數學推理和空間關係的測驗中，分數會比較高。

> *by contrast* 相較之下　　male (mel) *n.* 男性
> reasoning ('riznɪŋ) *n.* 推理
> spatial ('speʃəl) *adj.* 空間的

This seems to indicate that some differences are due to innate factors. 這似乎顯示，有些差異是由於先天性的因素。

> indicate ('ɪndə,ket) *v.* 顯示　　innate (ɪ'net) *adj.* 先天性的

But in some research papers, educational experiences or environmental influences seem to account for such variation.

但在某些研究報告中，教育經歷或環境的影響，似乎是造成這種差異的原因。

> *account for* 說明；是…的原因
> variation (,vɛrɪ'eʃən) *n.* 差異

[3](D) With no data concerning the superiority of male intelligence over the female, we had better accept the answer: "It depends."

由於沒有任何相關資料顯示，男性比女性聰明，所以我們最好接受這個答案：「智力是視情況而定的。」

> data〔'detə〕*n. pl.* 資料
> concerning〔kən'sɜnɪŋ〕*prep.* 有關
> superiority〔sə,pɪrɪ'ɔrətɪ〕*n.* 優秀
> ***It depends.*** 視情況而定。

A study has revealed that twins usually have similar IQs even if brought up in different environments. But according to some opposing data, environment is supposed to affect the development of intellectual powers.

有項研究顯示，雙胞胎即使是在不同的環境下被撫養長大，通常智商還是差不多。但是根據某些相反的資料顯示，環境被認為是影響智力發展的因素。

> reveal〔rɪ'vil〕*v.* 顯示　　***bring up*** 撫養長大
> opposing〔ə'pozɪŋ〕*adj.* 相反的；對立的
> suppose〔sə'poz〕*v.* 認為
> intellectual〔,ɪntḷ'ɛktʃʊəl〕*adj.* 智力的
> ***intellectual power*** 智力

[4](C) So, we cannot say intelligence is genetic or environmental in origin. Even scientific investigation fails to provide a definite answer. The reason is that there is no satisfactory definition of intelligence.

所以，我們不能說遺傳或環境就是影響智力的因素。甚至是科學研究也無法提供確切的答案。原因在於，智力並沒有令人滿意的定義。

genetic (dʒə'nɛtɪk) *adj.* 遺傳的　　origin ('ɔrədʒɪn) *n.* 起源
investigation (ɪn,vɛstə'geʃən) *n.* 調查；研究
fail to V. 無法~　　provide (prə'vaɪd) *v.* 提供
definite ('dɛfənɪt) *n.* 確切的
satisfactory (,sætɪs'fæktərɪ) *adj.* 令人滿意的；適合的
definition (,dɛfə'nɪʃən) *n.* 定義

Besides, we cannot cope with the limitations of research design. For example, we cannot put two people who apparently have different genes in identical environments.
此外，我們無法處理研究計劃的限制問題。舉例來說，我們無法把兩個基因顯然不同的人，放在完全相同的環境下。

cope with 應付；處理　　limitation (,lɪmə'teʃən) *n.* 限制
design (dɪ'zaɪn) *n.* 計劃
apparently (ə'pɛrəntlɪ) *adv.* 明顯地
gene (dʒin) *n.* 基因　　identical (aɪ'dɛntɪkḷ) *adj.* 完全相同的

[5](A) Nor can we forcibly put identical twins in different environments for the research. Therefore, the question remains unanswered.
我們也無法為了做研究，而強迫同卵雙胞胎待在不同的環境。因此，這個問題仍然無解。

forcibly ('fɔrsəblɪ) *adv.* 強迫地
identical twins 同卵雙胞胎　　remain (rɪ'men) *v.* 仍然
unanswered (ʌn'ænsəd) *adj.* 無回答的

TEST 28

說明： 第 1 至 5 題，每題一個空格。請依文意在文章後所提供的 (A) 到 (E) 選項中分別選出最適當者。

Yoga, a Sanskrit word for "union," means an experience of oneness or union with your inner being. ___1___ Integrated mind and body control leads to ultimate physical health and the achievement of mental tranquility.

The whole system of yoga is built on three main components: exercise, breathing, and meditation. The exercises of yoga are designed to put pressure on the glandular system of the body, thereby increasing its efficiency. The body is looked upon as the primary instrument that enables us to work and evolve in the world, and so a yoga student treats it with great care and respect. ___2___ A yoga student learns to control his/her breathing to improve the health and function of body and mind. These exercises prepare the body and mind for meditation, and the student can easily reach a state of mind that allows relief from everyday stress. ___3___

Yoga is suitable for most adults of any age or physical condition. ___4___ Yoga is not recommended for children under sixteen because their bodies' nervous and glandular systems are still growing. However, children may safely practice meditation and simple breathing exercises as long as they never hold their breath. ___5___ Children trained in these techniques are better able to manage anger and cope with stressful events. 【中正高中期中考】

(A) These techniques can greatly help children learn to relax, concentrate, and reduce impulsiveness.

(B) This union is the mind uniting with the body to attain a higher level of consciousness.

(C) Regular practice of all three parts of yoga produces a clear mind and capable body.

(D) Because of the non-strenuous nature of yoga, even those with physical limits can enjoy its benefits.

(E) Breathing techniques are based on the concept that breath is the source of life.

TEST 28 詳解

Yoga, a Sanskrit word for "union," means an experience of oneness or union with your inner being.

瑜珈，是「結合」這個字的梵文，意思是和你的內心合而爲一，或是結爲一體的經驗。

> yoga〔'jogə〕*n.* 瑜珈　　Sanskrit〔'sænskrɪt〕*n.* 梵文
> union〔'junjən〕*n.* 結合（爲一體）　　mean〔min〕*v.* 意思是
> experience〔ɪk'spɪrɪəns〕*n.* 體驗；經驗
> oneness〔'wʌnnɪs〕*n.* 一體；完整
> inner〔'ɪnə〕*adj.* 內在的；精神上的　　being〔'biɪŋ〕*n.* 本質；身心
> ***inner being*** 內心；心底

[1](**B**) <u>This union is the mind uniting with the body to attain a higher level of consciousness.</u> Integrated mind and body control leads to ultimate physical health and the achievement of mental tranquility.

這樣的結合，是身體與心靈合爲一體，而讓意識達到更高的層次。協調的身心控管，可以使身體達到最健康的狀態，而且還能達到心靈的平靜。

> mind〔maɪnd〕*n.* 心；精神；頭腦
> unite〔ju'naɪt〕*v.* 結合；合爲一體　　attain〔ə'ten〕*v.* 達到
> level〔'lɛvl̩〕*n.* 程度；階層
> consciousness〔'kɑnʃəsnɪs〕*n.* 意識；感覺
> integrated〔'ɪntə,gretɪd〕*adj.* 完整的；互相協調的
> control〔kən'trol〕*n.* 控制；管理　　***lead to*** 導致
> ultimate〔'ʌltəmɪt〕*adj.* 極點的；最大限度的
> physical〔'fɪzɪkl̩〕*adj.* 身體的　　health〔hɛlθ〕*n.* 健康
> achievement〔ə'tʃivmənt〕*n.* 達成　　mental〔'mɛntl̩〕*adj.* 心理的
> tranquility〔træŋ'kwɪlətɪ〕*n.* 平靜

The whole system of yoga is built on three main components: exercise, breathing, and meditation. The exercises of yoga are designed to put pressure on the glandular system of the body, thereby increasing its efficiency.

瑜珈的整個體系都是建立在三大要素上：運動、呼吸和冥想。在運動方面，瑜珈的設計，是爲了向身體裡面的淋巴系統施壓，以提高其運作效率。

system ('sıstəm) *n.* 體系　　main (men) *adj.* 主要的
component (kəm'ponənt) *n.* 構成要素
exercise ('ɛksɚˌsaɪz) *n.* 運動　　breathing ('briðɪŋ) *n.* 呼吸
meditation (ˌmɛdə'teʃən) *n.* 冥想　　design (dɪ'zaɪn) *v.* 設計
pressure ('prɛʃɚ) *n.* 壓　　glandular ('glændʒəlɚ) *adj.* 淋巴腺的
thereby (ðɛr'baɪ) *adv.* 藉以　　efficiency (ə'fɪʃənsɪ) *n.* 效率

The body is looked upon as the primary instrument that enables us to work and evolve in the world, and so a yoga student treats it with great care and respect.

身體被視爲使我們能在這個世界上工作和發展的主要工具，所以，學瑜珈的人會很小心謹愼地對待自己的身體。

be looked upon as 被視爲　　primary ('praɪˌmɛrɪ) *adj.* 主要的
instrument ('ɪnstrəmənt) *n.* 工具　　enable (ɪn'ebl̩) *v.* 使能夠
evolve (ɪ'vɑlv) *v.* 發展；進化　　treat (trit) *v.* 對待
with care 小心地　　respect (rɪ'spɛkt) *n.* 尊重
with respect 以愼重態度

[2](E) Breathing techniques are based on the concept that breath is the source of life. A yoga student learns to control his/her breathing to improve the health and function of body and mind.

呼吸技巧的理論基礎，即呼吸是生命的泉源。爲了改善身心健康與功能，學瑜珈的人要學習調節自己的呼吸。

technique〔tɛkˈnik〕*n.* 技巧　　***be based on*** 根據；以～爲基礎
concept〔ˈkɑnsɛpt〕*n.* 概念；理論　　breath〔brɛθ〕*n.* 呼吸
source〔sors〕*n.* 根源；泉源　　control〔kənˈtrol〕*v.* 控制；調節
improve〔ɪmˈpruv〕*v.* 改善　　function〔ˈfʌŋkʃən〕*n.* 功能

These exercises prepare the body and mind for meditation, and the student can easily reach a state of mind that allows relief from everyday stress. [3](C) Regular practice of all three parts of yoga produces a clear mind and capable body.

這種訓練可以讓學生的身心準備好冥想，然後輕易地達到可以消除日常壓力的精神狀態。規律地練習瑜珈的三大部分，會使你的頭腦清楚，身體更有力量。

prepare〔prɪˈpɛr〕*v.* 使…做準備　　***a state of mind*** 精神狀態；心態
allow〔əˈlaʊ〕*v.* 讓；允許　　relief〔rɪˈlif〕*n.* 解除；消除
everyday〔ˈɛvrɪˈde〕*adj.* 日常的　　stress〔strɛs〕*n.* 壓力
regular〔ˈrɛgjələ〕*adj.* 規律的　　produce〔prəˈdjus〕*v.* 製造；產生
clear〔klɪr〕*adj.* 清楚的　　capable〔ˈkepəbḷ〕*adj.* 有力量的

Yoga is suitable for most adults of any age or physical condition. [4](D) Because of the non-strenuous nature of yoga, even those with physical limits can enjoy its benefits.

大多數的成人都適合練瑜珈，不管年齡大小或身體狀況如何。因爲瑜珈的本質就是不用花力氣，所以甚至是在身體上面有限制的人，都可以享受它所帶來的好處。

suitable〔ˈsutəbḷ〕*adj.* 適合的　　adult〔əˈdʌlt〕*n.* 成人
condition〔kənˈdɪʃən〕*n.* 狀況　　strenuous〔ˈstrɛnjʊəs〕*adj.* 費力的
nature〔ˈnetʃə〕*n.* 本質　　limit〔ˈlɪmɪt〕*n.* 限制
benefit〔ˈbɛnəfɪt〕*n.* 好處

Yoga is not recommended for children under sixteen because their bodies' nervous and glandular systems are still growing. However, children may safely practice meditation and simple breathing exercises as long as they never hold their breath.

我們不建議十六歲以下的小孩練瑜珈，因為他們體內的神經系統和淋巴系統都還在發育。但是，只要孩子們不要閉氣，那麼也可以安全地練習冥想，還有簡單的呼吸訓練。

  recommend〔ˌrɛkə'mɛnd〕*v.* 推薦；建議
  nervous〔'nɝvəs〕*adj.* 神經的 grow〔gro〕*v.* 成長
  safely〔'seflɪ〕*adv.* 安全地
  simple〔'sɪmpḷ〕*adj.* 簡單的 ***as long as*** 只要
  hold〔hold〕*v.* 壓抑；抑住 ***hold*** *one's* ***breath*** 閉氣；屏息

[5](A) These techniques can greatly help children learn to relax, concentrate, and reduce impulsiveness. Children trained in these techniques are better able to manage anger and cope with stressful events.

這些技巧對於孩子們學習放鬆、專心，和減少衝動上，都有很大的幫助。受過這些技巧訓練的孩子們，都更能控制憤怒，以及應付壓力沉重的事件。

  greatly〔'gretlɪ〕*adv.* 大大地；非常地
  relax〔rɪ'læks〕*v.* 放鬆
  concentrate〔'kɑnsṇˌtret〕*v.* 專心 reduce〔rɪ'djus〕*v.* 減少
  impulsiveness〔ɪm'pʌlsɪvnɪs〕*n.* 衝動
  train〔tren〕*v.* 訓練 ***be better able to V.*** 更能夠～
  manage〔'mænɪdʒ〕*v.* 控制；處理 anger〔'æŋgɚ〕*n.* 憤怒
  cope with 應付；處理 stressful〔'strɛsfəl〕*adj.* 壓力重的
  event〔ɪ'vɛnt〕*n.* 事件

TEST 29

說明： 第 1 至 5 題，每題一個空格。請依文意在文章後所提供的 (A) 到 (E) 選項中分別選出最適當者。

Since Benjamin Franklin included the proverb "Early to bed and early to rise makes a man healthy, wealthy and wise" in his Poor Richard's Almanac, Americans have looked at sleeping habits as a measure of a person's character. ___1___

"I am an early riser, I'm achievement driven, and oh, my, has it served me well in the business world," said Otto Kroeger, a motivational speaker and business consultant in Virginia. ___2___ The writer Cynthia Ozick, who goes to bed after 3 a.m. and wakes up sometime after noon, said she lives with constant disapproval. "I am a creature of bad habits in the eyes of the world," she said. ___3___ As research shows, the time one wakes up has little bearing on income or success. Besides, people's sleep cycles are not entirely under their control.

___4___ "These are night owls who have just had their fill of people making them feel guilty and of other people who rag on them," said Carolyn Schur, a late sleeper, who advocates for night owls in speeches and in her book "Birds of a Different Feather." __5__ Researchers believe that about 10 percent of the population are extreme larks, 10 percent are extreme owls and the remaining 80 percent are somewhere in between. And they say the most important factor in determining to which group a person belongs is not ambition, but DNA. 【松山高中期末考】

(A) Scientists call the early risers larks, and the late sleepers owls.

(B) Buoyed by the reassessment of their bedtime habits, a few outspoken and well-rested late sleepers are speaking out against sleep prejudice.

(C) He routinely rises at 4 a.m., and preaches about the advantages of getting up before dawn to audiences and clients.

(D) Perhaps because in the agrarian past people had to wake at dawn to get in a full day's work outside, late sleepers have been viewed as a drag on the collective good.

(E) But sleep researchers are casting doubt on the presumed virtue and benefits of waking early.

TEST 29 詳解

Since Benjamin Franklin included the proverb "Early to bed and early to rise makes a man healthy, wealthy and wise" in his Poor Richard's Almanac, Americans have looked at sleeping habits as a measure of a person's character.

自從班哲明・富蘭克林把「早睡早起使人健康、富裕，又聰明」這句諺語，放進「窮人理查的年曆」一書後，美國人就把睡眠習慣，視爲衡量他人品德的標準。

> Benjamin Franklin (ˈbɛndʒəmən ˈfræŋklɪn) *n.* 班哲明・富蘭克林
> include (ɪnˈklud) *v.* 將～包含於…裡面
> proverb (ˈprɑvɝb) *n.* 諺語　　rise (raɪz) *v.* 起來；起床
> wealthy (ˈwɛlθɪ) *adj.* 富有的　　almanac (ˈɔlməˌnæk) *n.* 年曆
> measure (ˈmɛʒɚ) *n.* 標準　　character (ˈkærɪktɚ) *n.* 品德；性格

[1](D) Perhaps because in the agrarian past people had to wake at dawn to get in a full day's work outside, late sleepers have been viewed as a drag on the collective good.

也許是因爲以前農業社會的人，一整天都要在外面工作，所以必須在黎明時就醒來，而晚起的人，就會被視爲拖累團體利益的人。

> agrarian (əˈgrɛrɪən) *adj.* 農業的　　past (pæst) *n.* 過去
> wake (wek) *v.* 醒來　　dawn (dɔn) *n.* 黎明
> ***get in*** 參加；加入　　***late sleeper*** 晚起的人
> ***be viewed as*** 被視爲　　drag (dræg) *n.* 累贅；阻礙物
> collective (kəˈlɛktɪv) *adj.* 集體的；團體的　　good (gud) *n.* 利益

"I am an early riser, I'm achievement driven, and oh, my, has it served me well in the business world," said Otto Kroeger, a motivational speaker and business consultant in Virginia.

「我是個早起的人，我是一個被成就所驅策的人，噢！天啊！這樣
做對我的事業確實很有幫助，」奧圖・克羅格說，他是維吉尼亞州一名
善於激勵人的演講者，而且也是一位商業顧問。

riser (ˈraɪzɚ) *n.* 起床者　　***early riser*** 早起的人
achievement (əˈtʃivmənt) *n.* 成就；事業
drive (draɪv) *v.* 驅策　　my (maɪ) *interj.* 天啊
serve (sɝv) *v.* 幫助；對…有用　　***business world*** 事業；商業
motivational (ˌmotəˈveʃənḷ) *adj.* 激發性的；誘導的
consultant (kənˈsʌltənt) *n.* 顧問

[2](C) He routinely rises at 4 a.m., and preaches about the advantages
of getting up before dawn to audiences and clients. The writer
Cynthia Ozick, who goes to bed after 3 a.m. and wakes up sometime
after noon, said she lives with constant disapproval.

他每天都在早上四點鐘醒來，而且會對聽眾和顧客，竭力鼓吹在黎明之
前醒來的好處。作家辛西亞・奧斯克則是每天凌晨三點以後才睡，然後
中午過後才醒來，她說自己不斷忍受責難。

routinely (ruˈtinlɪ) *adv.* 日常地；慣例地
preach (pritʃ) *v.* 說教；竭力鼓吹
advantage (ədˈvæntɪdʒ) *n.* 優點
audience (ˈɔdɪəns) *n.* 聽眾
client (ˈklaɪənt) *n.* 客戶　　***live with*** 忍受
constant (ˈkɑnstənt) *adj.* 不斷的
disapproval (ˌdɪsəˈpruvḷ) *n.* 譴責；非難

"I am a creature of bad habits in the eyes of the world," she said.
[3](E) But sleep researchers are casting doubt on the presumed virtue
and benefits of waking early.

「在世人的眼裡，我是個生活習慣不好的人，」她說。但是研究睡眠的人，對於我們推測早起可能會有的優點和好處，開始感到懷疑。

creature〔'kritʃɚ〕*n.* 人；傢伙　　habit〔'hæbɪt〕*n.* 習慣
the world 世人　　researcher〔rɪ'sɜtʃɚ〕*n.* 研究人員
cast〔kæst〕*v.* 把…加（於）　　***cast doubt on*** 懷疑
presumed〔prɪ'zumd〕*adj.* 假定的；推測的
virtue〔'vɜtʃʊ〕*n.* 美德；優點　　benefit〔'bɛnəfɪt〕*n.* 好處

As research shows, the time one wakes up has little bearing on income or success. Besides, people's sleep cycles are not entirely under their control.

研究顯示，一個人醒來的時間和收入或成就，並沒有什麼關係。此外，人們的睡眠週期，並不是完全由自己來掌控的。

research〔rɪ'sɜtʃ〕*n.* 研究　　bearing〔'bɛrɪŋ〕*n.* 關係
income〔'ɪn,kʌm〕*n.* 收入　　cycle〔'saɪk!〕*n.* 週期
entirely〔ɪn'taɪrlɪ〕*adv.* 完全地　　control〔kən'trol〕*n.* 控制

[4](B) Buoyed by the reassessment of their bedtime habits, a few outspoken and well-rested late sleepers are speaking out against sleep prejudice.

受到重新評估就寢習慣的鼓勵，有些坦率且精力充沛的晚起者，大膽地說出他們反對睡眠歧視。

buoy〔bɔɪ〕*v.* 鼓勵　　reassessment〔,riə'sɛsmənt〕*n.* 重新評估
bedtime〔'bɛd,taɪm〕*n.* 就寢時間
outspoken〔'aʊt'spokən〕*adj.* 坦率的
well-rested〔'wɛl'rɛstɪd〕*adj.* 精力充沛的
speak out 大膽地說出　　against〔ə'gɛnst〕*prep.* 反對
prejudice〔'prɛdʒədɪs〕*n.* 歧視

"These are night owls who have just had their fill of people making them feel guilty and of other people who rag on them," said Carolyn Schur, a late sleeper, who advocates for night owls in speeches and in her book "Birds of a Different Feather."

「這些夜貓子，已經受夠了讓他們感到內疚的人，還有責罵他們的人，」卡洛琳・修爾這麼說，她也是個晚起的人，她在演講以及「擁有不同羽毛的鳥」一書中，提倡要當個夜貓子。

owl〔aʊl〕*n.* 貓頭鷹　　***night owl*** 熬夜的人；夜貓子
have had *one's **fill of*** 飽嚐…；對…生膩
guilty〔'gɪltɪ〕*adj.* 內疚的；心虛的　　rag〔ræg〕*v.* 責罵
advocate〔'ædvə͵ket〕*v.* 提倡；主張　　feather〔'fɛðɚ〕*n.* 羽毛

[5](A) Scientists call the early risers larks, and the late sleepers owls. Researchers believe that about 10 percent of the population are extreme larks, 10 percent are extreme owls and the remaining 80 percent are somewhere in between.

科學家稱早起的人為雲雀，而晚起的人則是貓頭鷹。研究人員認為，約有百分之十的人，是非常早起的人，百分之十的人非常晚起，而剩下的百分之八十，則是介於中間。

scientist〔'saɪəntɪst〕*n.* 科學家　　lark〔lɑrk〕*n.* 雲雀
percent〔pɚ'sɛnt〕*n.* 百分之…　　population〔͵pɑpjə'leʃən〕*n.* 人口
extreme〔ɪk'strim〕*adj.* 極度的；非常的
remaining〔rɪ'menɪŋ〕*adj.* 剩下的　　***in between*** 在中間

And they say the most important factor in determining to which group a person belongs is not ambition, but DNA.

他們還說，決定一個人屬於哪一個群體的最大因素，不是這個人的抱負，而是他的 DNA。

determine〔dɪ'tɜmɪn〕*v.* 決定　　belong〔bə'lɔŋ〕*v.* 屬於
ambition〔æm'bɪʃən〕*n.* 抱負；追求的目標　　***DNA*** 去氧核醣核酸

TEST 30

說明： 第 1 至 5 題，每題一個空格。請依文意在文章後所提供的 (A) 到 (E) 選項中分別選出最適當者。

Guy de Maupassant is generally considered the greatest French short story writer. His tales are marked by objectivity, a highly controlled style, and sometimes sheer comedy. ___1___ According to Maupassant, a modern novel aims at forcing us to think and understand the deeper, hidden meaning of events. For example, the point of his short story "The Necklace" is that vanity and pride go before a fall. ___2___ She felt she could not attend the Minister's party without a stylish dress and expensive jewels. ___3___ As a result, she suffered for ten years.

It seemed that Matilda did not learn what had caused her hardship because she still would daydream about how beautiful and admired she was at the ball, instead of realizing how vain and silly she had been. ___4___ Her pride led her to conceal the fact from her friend. Instead of seeing her ruination as being her own fault, Matilda considered it a cruel trick of fate. ___5___

【台南女中期中考】

(A) We readers, on the contrary, see clearly that her vanity led her to seek to borrow the necklace.

(B) However, we learn from this story that unrealistic desires to change one's fate may bring great sorrow and hardship.

(C) The main character, Matilda, was vain so she was dissatisfied with her life.

(D) Besides, she did not tell Mrs. Forestier about the loss of the necklace because she was too proud and maybe too frightened.

(E) Usually they were built around simple episodes from everyday life, which revealed the hidden sides of people.

TEST 30 詳解

Guy de Maupassant is generally considered the greatest French short story writer. His tales are marked by objectivity, a highly controlled style, and sometimes sheer comedy.

一般認為，莫泊桑是法國最偉大的短篇小說家。他的故事以客觀性為特色，風格非常節制，有時候還會出現喜劇。

Guy de Maupassant ('gidə 'mopə,sɑnt) *n.* 莫泊桑
（ 1850-93，法國作家 ）
generally ('dʒɛnərəlɪ) *adv.* 一般地；通常
consider (kən'sɪdə) *v.* 認為；視為
story ('storɪ) *n.* 短篇小說　　tale (tel) *n.* 故事
mark (mɑrk) *v.* 使具有…特色　***be marked by*** 特色是
objectivity (,ɑbdʒɛk'tɪvətɪ) *n.* 客觀性
highly ('haɪlɪ) *adv.* 非常
controlled (kən'trold) *adj.* 受制的；有節制的
style (staɪl) *n.* 風格　　sheer (ʃɪr) *adj.* 完全的；全然的
comedy ('kɑmədɪ) *n.* 喜劇

[1](E) Usually they were built around simple episodes from everyday life, which revealed the hidden sides of people. According to Maupassant, a modern novel aims at forcing us to think and understand the deeper, hidden meaning of events.
那些故事通常是圍繞著日常生活的簡單情節發展，而且會透露出人類隱藏起來的那一面。根據莫泊桑的說法，現代小說的目標，就是要強迫我們思考，以了解隱藏在事件背後更深一層的意義。

build〔 bɪld 〕*v.* 建立;發展

simple〔'sɪmpl̩〕*adj.* 簡單的

episode〔'ɛpə,sod〕*n.* 插曲;一段(情節)

reveal〔rɪ'vil〕*v.* 透露　hidden〔'hɪdn̩〕*adj.* (被)隱藏的

side〔saɪd〕*n.* 面　*according to* 根據

modern〔'modən〕*adj.* 現代的　novel〔'novl̩〕*n.* 小說

aim at 目的在於　force〔fors〕*v.* 強迫

deep〔dip〕*adj.* 深的　meaning〔'minɪŋ〕*n.* 意義

event〔ɪ'vɛnt〕*n.* 事件

For example, the point of his short story "The Necklace" is that
vanity and pride go before a fall. [2](C) The main character, Matilda,
was vain so she was dissatisfied with her life.

例如,他的短篇小說「項鍊」,重點就是在描寫虛榮和驕傲會導致失敗。
主角馬蒂達很愛慕虛榮,所以她不滿意自己的生活。

point〔pɔɪnt〕*n.* 重點　necklace〔'nɛklɪs〕*n.* 項鍊

vanity〔'vænətɪ〕*n.* 虛榮心　pride〔praɪd〕*n.* 驕傲

fall〔fɔl〕*n.* 跌倒;墮落;衰落

main〔men〕*adj.* 主要的

character〔'kærɪktə〕*n.* 角色;人物

vain〔ven〕*adj.* 虛榮的

dissatisfied〔dɪs'sætɪs,faɪd〕*adj.* 不滿意的

She felt she could not attend the Minister's party without a stylish
dress and expensive jewels. [3](A) We readers, on the contrary, see
clearly that her vanity led her to seek to borrow the necklace. As
a result, she suffered for ten years.

她覺得如果沒有時髦的洋裝和昂貴的珠寶，就無法參加部長的宴會。相反地，我們這些讀者都很清楚地知道，她的虛榮心使她試圖去借那條項鍊。結果，她因此而受了十年的苦。

attend〔ə'tɛnd〕*v.* 參加　　minister〔'mɪnɪstɚ〕*n.* 部長

stylish〔'staɪlɪʃ〕*adj.* 時髦的；漂亮的

dress〔drɛs〕*n.* 洋裝　　jewel〔'dʒuəl〕*n.* 珠寶

contrary〔'kɑntrɛrɪ〕*n.* 相反的事物

on the contrary 相反地　　see〔si〕*v.* 知道

clearly〔'klɪrlɪ〕*adv.* 清楚地

lead *sb.* ***to V.*** 使某人～　　seek〔sik〕*v.* 試圖

borrow〔'bɑro〕*v.* 借（入）

as a result 因此；結果　　suffer〔'sʌfɚ〕*v.* 受苦

It seemed that Matilda did not learn what had caused her hardship because she still would daydream about how beautiful and admired she was at the ball, instead of realzing how vain and silly she had been.

　　馬蒂達似乎不了解使她受苦的原因，因為她仍然會幻想，在那場舞會中，自己有多美，有多令人欽佩，卻不知道自己有多虛榮和愚蠢。

seem〔sim〕*v.* 似乎　　cause〔kɔz〕*v.*（給人）帶來

hardship〔'hɑrdʃɪp〕*n.* 艱難；辛苦

daydream〔'de,drim〕*v.* 幻想

admired〔əd'maɪrd〕*adj.* 令人欽佩的

ball〔bɔl〕*n.* 舞會　　***instead of*** 而不是

realize〔'riə,laɪz〕*v.* 了解；知道

silly〔'sɪlɪ〕*adj.* 愚蠢的

[4](D) Besides, she did not tell Mrs. Forestier about the loss of the necklace because she was too proud and maybe too frightened. Her pride led her to conceal the fact from her friend.

另外，她沒有跟佛瑞絲蒂爾太太說項鍊不見的事，因為她太驕傲，而且可能也太害怕。她的驕傲使她隱瞞事實，不讓朋友知道。

loss〔lɔs〕*n.* 遺失　　proud〔praud〕*adj.* 驕傲的
frightened〔'fraɪtn̩d〕*adj.* 感到害怕的
conceal〔kən'sil〕*v.* 隱藏；隱瞞
conceal sth. *from* sb. 對某人隱瞞某事
fact〔fækt〕*n.* 事實

Instead of seeing her ruination as being her own fault, Matilda considered it a cruel trick of fate. [5](B) However, we learn from this story that unrealistic desires to change one's fate may bring great sorrow and hardship.

馬蒂達認為破產不是她的錯，她認為這是命運的無情捉弄。但是，從這個故事中，我們學到了，不切實際地幻想要改變命運，可能會帶來許多悲傷和苦難。

see〔si〕*v.* 視為；認為
see A *as* B 認為 A 是 B
ruination〔͵ruɪn'eʃən〕*n.* 破產；衰敗
fault〔fɔlt〕*n.* 過錯　　cruel〔'kruəl〕*adj.* 殘忍的；無情的
trick〔trɪk〕*n.* 開玩笑；捉弄　　fate〔fet〕*n.* 命運
unrealistic〔͵ʌnrɪə'lɪstɪk〕*adj.* 不切實際的
desire〔dɪ'zaɪr〕*n.* 想要；渴望　　sorrow〔'saro〕*n.* 悲傷

TEST 31

說明： 第 1 至 5 題，每題一個空格。請依文意在文章後所提供的 (A) 到
(E) 選項中分別選出最適當者。

The world's largest weather system is over the
Pacific Ocean. There is a high-pressure system over
the Eastern Pacific. This causes winds to blow toward
the wet low-pressure system over Indonesia. All of this
causes the ocean currents to move toward the west.
___1___

Every four to ten years, something happens to this
weather system. Everything changes, and scientists
don't understand why. The low-pressure area moves
toward the east, the high-pressure area is very weak,
and the winds blow toward the east. A great pile of
warm surface water moves toward South America.
People call this "El Niño." ___2___

Usually the effects of El Niño are very mild.
However, the one that started in 1982 was different
from the other recent ones. It had a very powerful
effect on the world's climate. It caused huge changes
in the ocean currents. ___3___ There were terrible

windstorms and huge ocean waves. These waves swept houses into the sea. El Niño did billions of dollars worth of damage. ___4___

In 1983, the winds, ocean currents, and pressure areas started to become normal again. Meanwhile, scientists throughout the world organized research to learn more about El Niño. ___5___ It is a very complicated problem, but if the scientists of the world work together, they should be able to learn the causes of El Niño. Then they will be able to predict what will happen and work to prevent a repeat of the death and destruction of 1982-1983. 【師大附中期中考】

(A) It caused floods in some areas and droughts in others.

(B) They are using satellites and research boats to observe the atmosphere and the ocean.

(C) These currents cause warm water to pile up in the Western Pacific.

(D) It usually happens at Christmas time, and El Niño is the Spanish name for the baby Jesus.

(E) Thousands of people lost their lives and thousands of others were left homeless.

TEST 31 詳解

The world's largest weather system is over the Pacific Ocean. There is a high-pressure system over the Eastern Pacific. This causes winds to blow toward the wet low-pressure system over Indonesia.

世界上最大的天氣系統，是位於太平洋上方。在東太平洋上面，有個高壓系統。該系統使風吹向印尼上方的潮濕低壓系統。

weather ('wɛðɚ) *n.* 天氣　　*weather system* 天氣系統
Pacific (pə'sɪfɪk) *adj.* 太平洋的　　*Pacific Ocean* 太平洋
pressure ('prɛʃɚ) *n.* 壓力；氣壓
high-pressure ('haɪ'prɛʃɚ) *adj.* 高壓的
eastern ('istən) *adj.* 東部的　　cause (kɔz) *v.* 使
wind (wɪnd) *n.* 風　　blow (blo) *v.* 吹
toward (tə'wɔrd) *prep.* 朝向　　wet (wɛt) *adj.* 潮濕的
low-pressure ('lo'prɛʃɚ) *adj.* 低壓的
Indonesia (ˌɪndo'niʃə) *n.* 印尼共和國

All of this causes the ocean currents to move toward the west. [1](C) These currents cause warm water to pile up in the Western Pacific.
以上這些現象使洋流向西移動。而這些洋流會使溫暖的海水都積聚在西太平洋。

ocean ('oʃən) *n.* 海洋　　current ('kɝənt) *n.* 海流
ocean current 洋流　　west (wɛst) *n.* 西方　　pile (paɪl) *v.* 堆積
pile up 累積；積聚　　western ('wɛstən) *adj.* 西部的

Every four to ten years, something happens to this weather system. Everything changes, and scientists don't understand why. The low-pressure area moves toward the east, the high-pressure area is very weak, and the winds blow toward the east.

　　每隔四到十年，這個天氣系統就會有所變化。一切都會改變，而且
科學家不知道原因何在。低壓區向東移動，高壓區變得很脆弱，所以風
往東邊吹。

　　scientist (ˈsaɪəntɪst) n. 科學家　　area (ˈɛrɪə) n. 區域
　　move (muv) v. 移動　　east (ist) n. 東方
　　weak (wik) adj. 脆弱的

A great pile of warm surface water moves toward South America.
People call this "El Niño." **²(D) It usually happens at Christmas
time, and El Niño is the Spanish name for the baby Jesus.**
海面上有大量溫暖的海水流向南美洲。人們稱之為「聖嬰現象」。它通
常發生在聖誕節的時候，而厄爾尼諾則是耶穌嬰兒時期的西班牙名稱。

　　pile (paɪl) n. 許多；大量　　*a pile of* 大量的；很多的
　　surface (ˈsɜfɪs) adj. 表面的；水面上的
　　El Niño (ɛlˈninjo) n. 厄爾尼諾現象；聖嬰現象
　　Christmas (ˈkrɪsməs) adj. 聖誕節的
　　Spanish (ˈspænɪʃ) adj. 西班牙的
　　Jesus (ˈdʒizəs) n. 耶穌

　　Usually the effects of El Niño are very mild. However, the
one that started in 1982 was different from the other recent ones.
It had a very powerful effect on the world's climate.
　　聖嬰現象的影響通常很輕微。但是從一九八二年起的聖嬰現象，
卻和最近這幾次的有所不同。它對全世界的氣候造成很大的影響。

　　effect (ɪˈfɛkt) n. 影響　　mild (maɪld) adj. 溫和的
　　recent (ˈrisn̩t) adj. 最近的　　powerful (ˈpauəfəl) adj. 強大的
　　climate (ˈklaɪmɪt) n. 氣候

It caused huge changes in the ocean currents. ³(A) It caused floods in some areas and droughts in others. There were terrible windstorms and huge ocean waves.

它使洋流產生巨大的變化。有些地區發生水災，有些發生旱災。它還造成可怕的風暴和巨浪。

cause〔kɔz〕v. 造成　　huge〔hjudʒ〕adj. 巨大的
flood〔flʌd〕n. 水災　　drought〔draut〕n. 旱災
terrible〔'tɛrəbl̩〕adj. 可怕的
windstorm〔'wɪnd,stɔrm〕n. 風暴　　wave〔wev〕n. 波浪

These waves swept houses into the sea. El Niño did billions of dollars worth of damage. ⁴(E) Thousands of people lost their lives and thousands of others were left homeless.

這些海浪把房屋沖進海裡。聖嬰現象造成了數十億的損失。有數以千計的人喪生，而且有數千人無家可歸。

sweep〔swip〕v. 掃；沖走（三態變化為：sweep-swept-swept）
billion〔'bɪljən〕n. 十億　　***billions of*** 數十億的
worth〔wɝθ〕n. 值…的分量
damage〔'dæmɪdʒ〕n. 損害；損失　　lose〔luz〕v. 失去
leave〔liv〕v. 使…處於某種狀態
homeless〔'homlɪs〕adj. 無家可歸的

In 1983, the winds, ocean currents, and pressure areas started to become normal again. Meanwhile, scientists throughout the world organized research to learn more about El Niño.

在一九八三年時，風、洋流和氣壓區，又開始恢復正常。這時，爲了更了解聖嬰現象，來自世界各地的科學家，組成了研究小組。

normal ('nɔrml) *adj.* 正常的
meanwhile ('min,hwaIl) *adv.* 這時
throughout (θru'aut) *prep.* 在…各處
throughout the world 在全世界的
organize ('ɔrgən,aIz) *v.* 組織；成立組織
research (rI's3tʃ , 'ris3tʃ) *n.* 研究；調查　　***learn about*** 知道

[5](B) <u>They are using satellites and research boats to observe the atmosphere and the ocean.</u> It is a very complicated problem, but if the scientists of the world work together, they should be able to learn the causes of El Niño.

他們利用人造衛星和調查船，來觀察大氣層和海洋。這是個很複雜的問題，但是如果全世界的科學家一起合作，應該就能得知聖嬰現象的成因。

satellite ('sætl,aIt) *n.* 人造衛星　　observe (əb'z3v) *v.* 觀察
atmosphere ('ætməs,fIr) *n.* 大氣層
complicated ('kɑmplə,ketId) *adj.* 複雜的　　***work together*** 合作
be able to V. 能夠　　cause (kɔz) *n.* 原因

Then they will be able to predict what will happen and work to prevent a repeat of the death and destruction of 1982-1983.

然後，他們就能預測即將發生的事，並努力預防一九八二年到一九八三年間的死亡和破壞重演。

predict (prI'dIkt) *v.* 預測　　prevent (prI'vɛnt) *v.* 預防
repeat (rI'pit) *n.* 重複發生　　destruction (dI'strʌkʃən) *n.* 破壞

TEST 32

說明： 第 1 至 5 題，每題一個空格。請依文意在文章後所提供的 (A) 到
(E) 選項中分別選出最適當者。

In Taiwan much time and energy are spent on
getting a proper education and finding a good job.
___1___ A new study by the Department of Health
in Taiwan shows that more than half of the adult
population in Taiwan lacks an understanding of
important health problems. ___2___ Surprisingly,
only 51 percent of the people surveyed understand
that the common cold has no cure. Colds are
caused by viruses, not bacteria, so taking medicine
has absolutely no use at all. ___3___ More than
two-thirds believe that it is only the nicotine in
cigarettes rather than the other chemicals that cause
cancer. ___4___ Since 26 percent of Taiwanese
adults smoke, such a misunderstanding will lead
to more illness, suffering, and early death. ___5___
The survey concludes that younger Taiwanese have

a better understanding of health concerns than
their parents, while senior citizens have the
least understanding among the three age groups.

【師大附中期中考】

(A) The problem is made worse by doctors
who give their patients large doses of
useless drugs.

(B) As a result, health concerns have been
neglected.

(C) But the outlook for health education in
Taiwan is not all negative.

(D) These people believe that if they smoke
"light" cigarettes with less nicotine,
they will not get cancer.

(E) More than 2,000 adults took part in the
survey to find out about their knowledge
of diet, healthcare, disease control, and
medication.

TEST 32 詳解

In Taiwan much time and energy are spent on getting a proper education and finding a good job. [1](B) As a result, health concerns have been neglected. A new study by the Department of Health in Taiwan shows that more than half of the adult population in Taiwan lacks an understanding of important health problems.

在台灣，許多時間和精力，都被用在受適當的教育，還有找到好工作上面。結果，和健康有關的事都被忽略了。台灣衛生署最新的研究顯示，台灣有超過一半的成人，對於重要的健康問題缺乏了解。

proper〔'prɑpɚ〕*adj.* 適當的　　*as a result* 因此；結果
concern〔kən'sɝn〕*n.* 相關的事　　neglect〔nɪ'glɛkt〕*v.* 忽視
the Department of Health 衛生署　　adult〔ə'dʌlt〕*adj.* 成人的
population〔ˌpɑpjə'leʃən〕*n.* 人口　　lack〔læk〕*v.* 缺乏

[2](E) More than 2,000 adults took part in the survey to find out about their knowledge of diet, healthcare, disease control, and medication. Surprisingly, only 51 percent of the people surveyed understand that the common cold has no cure. 有兩千多名成人參與了這項調查，以查出他們對於飲食、醫療、疾病管制，還有藥物的了解。令人驚訝的是，在接受調查的人當中，只有百分之五十一的人知道一般的感冒沒有特效藥。

take part in 參與　　survey〔sɚ've〕*n.* 調查；民意調查　*v.* 調查
healthcare〔'hɛlθ'kɛr〕*n.* 保健；醫療
disease〔dɪ'ziz〕*n.* 疾病　　control〔kən'trol〕*n.* 管制
medication〔ˌmɛdɪ'keʃən〕*n.* 藥物
common cold （普通的）感冒　　cure〔kjur〕*n.* 治療的藥物

Colds are caused by viruses, not bacteria, so taking medicine has absolutely no use at all. [3](A) The problem is made worse by doctors who give their patients large doses of useless drugs.

感冒是由病毒所引起的，不是細菌，所以吃藥絕對是完全無效。但是開很多沒用的藥給病人的醫生，卻使問題變得更嚴重。

virus〔'vaɪrəs〕*n.* 病毒　　bacteria〔bæk'tɪrɪə〕*n. pl.* 細菌
absolutely〔'æbsə,lutlɪ〕*adv.* 絕對地；完全地
dose〔dos〕*n.*（藥一次的）服用量

More than two-thirds believe that it is only the nicotine in cigarettes
rather than the other chemicals that cause cancer. <u>⁴(D) These people</u>
<u>believe that if they smoke "light" cigarettes with less nicotine, they</u>
<u>will not get cancer.</u>
有超過三分之二的人認為，香菸裡面只有尼古丁會致癌，而其他化學物質都
不會。這些人認為，如果他們抽尼古丁含量較低的「淡」菸，就不會得癌症。

> ***two-thirds*** 三分之二　　nicotine〔'nɪkə,tin〕*n.* 尼古丁
> ***rather than*** 而不是　　chemical〔'kɛmɪkl̩〕*n.* 化學物質

Since 26 percent of Taiwanese adults smoke, such a misunderstanding
will lead to more illness, suffering, and early death. <u>⁵(C) But the</u>
<u>outlook for health education in Taiwan is not all negative.</u>
因為台灣有百分之二十六的成人抽菸，所以這樣的誤解會導致更多疾病、更
多痛苦，還有早死。但是台灣健康教育的前景，並非一片黑暗。

> adult〔ə'dʌlt〕*n.* 成人
> misunderstanding〔,mɪsʌndɚ'stændɪŋ〕*n.* 誤解
> illness〔'ɪlnɪs〕*n.* 疾病　　suffering〔'sʌfərɪŋ〕*n.* 痛苦
> outlook〔'aʊt,lʊk〕*n.* 展望；前景
> negative〔'nɛɡətɪv〕*adj.* 負面的；不太好的

The survey concludes that younger Taiwanese have a better
understanding of health concerns than their parents, while senior
citizens have the least understanding among the three age groups.
這份調查的結論是，年輕一輩的台灣人，都比他們的父母還要了解和健康有
關的事，然而，老人則是三個年齡層中，最不了解健康的人。

> conclude〔kən'klud〕*v.* 下結論；斷定　　while〔hwaɪl〕*conj.* 然而
> ***senior citizen*** 老人　　***age group*** 年齡層

TEST 33

說明： 第 1 至 5 題，每題一個空格。請依文意在文章後所提供的 (A) 到 (E) 選項中分別選出最適當者。

For thousands of years, people have gazed up into space and wondered: What are the stars made of? What is it like in space? Is there any other life out there? We can answer some of these questions today, but "the final frontier" still holds many mysteries. ___1___ Making that dream come true, however, takes a lot of hard work.

When people first blasted off into space, all astronauts were former military pilots, and all were men. ___2___ Some are pilots, but others are scientists, doctors, engineers or chemists.

Aspiring astronauts must meet very strict requirements. ___3___ Of the thousands of people who apply to become astronauts each year, only about 100 people get accepted for astronaut training.

Once a person has been accepted into the space program, he or she undergoes a year of difficult training. ___4___ They practice everything from liftoff to landing. Safety and emergency procedures are an important part of their training, too. They practice solving problems that might occur while they are in space. ___5___ Since astronauts perform experiments in space, they need knowledge of many scientific fields. 【嘉義高中複習考】

(A) In addition, they take many scientific courses, including mathematics, computer science and astronomy.

(B) They must have excellent health, a college degree and three years of experience in their field.

(C) Astronaut candidates must learn about their spacecraft.

(D) Those who wish to solve these mysteries dream of becoming astronauts.

(E) These days, a variety of men and women train to become astronauts.

TEST 33 詳解

For thousands of years, people have gazed up into space and wondered: What are the stars made of? What is it like in space? Is there any other life out there?

數千年來,人們凝視著天空時,都會想:星星是由什麼構成的?太空長什麼樣子?那裡有其他的生物嗎?

gaze〔gez〕*v.* 凝視;注視　　space〔spes〕*n.* 太空
wonder〔'wʌndə〕*v.* 想知道　　*be made of* 由⋯製成
life〔laɪf〕*n.* 生物　　*out there* 在那邊

We can answer some of these questions today, but "the final frontier" still holds many mysteries. [1](D) Those who wish to solve these mysteries dream of becoming astronauts. Making that dream come true, however, takes a lot of hard work.

我們現在已經可以回答其中一些問題,但是「最後的邊疆」有很多地方還是個謎。那些想要解開謎題的人,都夢想成為太空人。但是,要非常努力,才能讓夢想成真。

frontier〔frʌn'tɪr〕*n.* 邊疆　　mystery〔'mɪstrɪ〕*n.* 謎;奧祕
astronaut〔'æstrə,nɔt〕*n.* 太空人　　*hard work* 努力

When people first blasted off into space, all astronauts were former military pilots, and all were men. [2](E) These days, a variety of men and women train to become astronauts. Some are pilots, but others are scientists, doctors, engineers or chemists.

人類第一次發射火箭進入太空時，所有的太空人，之前都是軍隊裡的飛行員，而且全部是男性。近來，各行各業的男性和女性，都被訓練成太空人。有些是飛行員，但有些是科學家、醫生、工程師，或化學家。

> ***blast off*** （火箭、飛彈等）發射升空；將（太空人等）用火箭送入太空　　**former** (ˈfɔrmɚ) *adj.* 前任的；從前的
> **military** (ˈmɪləˌtɛrɪ) *adj.* 軍隊的　　**pilot** (ˈpaɪlət) *n.* 飛行員
> ***a variety of*** 各種的；各式各樣的
> **engineer** (ˌɛndʒəˈnɪr) *n.* 工程師
> **chemist** (ˈkɛmɪst) *n.* 化學家

Aspiring astronauts must meet very strict requirements. [3](B)
<u>They must have excellent health, a college degree and three years</u>
<u>of experience in their field.</u>

有抱負的太空人，得符合非常嚴格的要求。他們必須要非常健康，要有學士學位，而且在其所學的領域中，要有三年的經驗。

> **aspiring** (əˈspaɪrɪŋ) *adj.* 胸懷大志的；有抱負的
> **meet** (mit) *v.* 符合　　**strict** (strɪkt) *adj.* 嚴格的
> **requirement** (rɪˈkwaɪrmənt) *n.* 要求；必備條件
> **degree** (dɪˈgri) *n.* 學位

Of the thousands of people who apply to become astronauts each
year, only about 100 people get accepted for astronaut training.
每年都有數千人來應徵要當太空人，但大約只有一百個人會被認可，
而得以接受太空人的訓練。

> **apply** (əˈplaɪ) *v.* 申請；應徵
> **accept** (əkˈsɛpt) *v.* 認可；接受
> **training** (ˈtrenɪŋ) *n.* 訓練

Once a person has been accepted into the space program, he or she undergoes a year of difficult training. [4](C) Astronaut candidates must learn about their spacecraft.

一旦被認可加入太空計劃，就要接受一年的艱苦訓練。太空人的候選人，必須要了解他們的太空船。

undergo〔ˌʌndə'go〕*v.* 經歷；接受
candidate〔'kændə,det〕*n.* 候選人　　***learn about*** 了解；明白
spacecraft〔'spes,kræft〕*n.* 太空船

They practice everything from liftoff to landing. Safety and emergency procedures are an important part of their training, too. They practice solving problems that might occur while they are in space.

他們要練習從發射到降落的每一件事。在他們的訓練中，安全措施和緊急措施也是很重要的部分。他們要練習解決在太空可能發生的問題。

liftoff〔'lɪft,ɔf〕*n.* 起飛；發射　　landing〔'lændɪŋ〕*n.* 降落
emergency〔ɪ'mɝdʒənsɪ〕*adj.* 緊急的
procedure〔prə'sidʒə〕*n.* 程序；措施

[5](A) In addition, they take many scientific courses, including mathematics, computer science and astronomy. Since astronauts perform experiments in space, they need knowledge of many scientific fields.

此外，他們要上很多理科的課程，包括數學、電腦科學，和天文學。因為太空人要在太空中做實驗，所以他們需要知道許多科學領域的知識。

scientific〔ˌsaɪən'tɪfɪk〕*adj.* 理科的；科學的
course〔kors〕*n.* 課程　　astronomy〔ə'strɑnəmɪ〕*n.* 天文學
perform〔pə'fɔrm〕*v.* 做；執行

TEST 34

說明：第 1 至 5 題，每題一個空格。請依文意在文章後所提供的 (A) 到
　　　(E) 選項中分別選出最適當者。

One of the most important advances in medicine is the
ability to transfuse blood. ___1___ It is because transfusions
make certain surgical procedures possible.

When a transfusion is needed and a life is saved, the doctors
are not the only heroes. ___2___ They have donated some of their
own blood. ___3___ They do not know the person who has received
it. They know only that they helped another human being.

The Red Cross runs a widely known blood program. A
person who wishes to donate blood can do so at a Red Cross center.
___4___ They screen out those whose blood may not be safe for
transfusion, and then a pint of blood is taken from the donor's
arm. ___5___ But a doughnut and a cup of coffee are enough to
put him quickly on his feet again. 〔北模〕

(A) Thanks to blood transfusions, countless lives are saved
　　each year.
(B) The donor may feel a little weak afterwards.
(C) Women and men in all occupations have made this
　　event possible.
(D) Trained staff interview each potential donor about his
　　or her health.
(E) That is, they have donated blood to a "blood bank."

TEST 34 詳解

One of the most important advances in medicine is the ability to transfuse blood.　[1](A) Thanks to blood transfusions, countless lives are saved each year.　It is because transfusions make certain surgical procedures possible.

輸血是醫學方面最重要的進步之一。因為輸血，使某些外科手術得以進行，所以每年都拯救了無數的生命。

advance (əd'væns) *n.* 進步　　transfuse (træns'fjuz) *v.* 輸 (血)
blood (blʌd) *n.* 血　　***thanks to*** 幸虧；由於
transfusion (træns'fjuʒən) *n.* 輸血
countless ('kauntlıs) *adj.* 無數的　　save (sev) *v.* 拯救
certain ('sɝtṇ) *adj.* 某些　　surgical ('sɝdʒıkḷ) *adj.* 外科手術的
procedure (prə'sidʒɚ) *n.* 程序　　***surgical procedure*** 外科手術

When a transfusion is needed and a life is saved, the doctors are not the only heroes.　[2](C) Women and men in all occupations have made this event possible.　They have donated some of their own blood.

當需要輸血，並因此而救回一條人命時，醫生並不是唯一的英雄。是來自各行各業的人造就了這件事。他們捐出自己部分的血液。

hero ('hıro) *n.* 英雄　　occupation (,ɑkjə'peʃən) *n.* 職業
event (ı'vɛnt) *n.* 事件　　donate ('donet) *v.* 捐贈

[3](E) That is, they have donated blood to a "blood bank."　They do not know the person who has received it.　They know only that they helped another human being.

也就是說，他們捐血給「血庫」。他們不知道是誰用了他們的血。他們只知道自己幫了另一個人。

> ***that is*** 也就是說　　　bank〔bæŋk〕*n.* 儲存所；庫
> ***blood bank*** 血庫　　　receive〔rɪ'siv〕*v.* 接受　　　***human being*** 人

The Red Cross runs a widely known blood program. A person who wishes to donate blood can do so at a Red Cross center. <u>⁴(D) Trained staff interview each potential donor about his or her health.</u>

紅十字會實施了一個廣為人知的捐血計劃。想捐血的人，可以到紅十字中心。受過訓練的工作人員，會審查可能捐血者的健康狀況。

> ***the Red Cross*** 紅十字會（慈善團體）　　　run〔rʌn〕*v.* 進行；實施
> ***widely known*** 廣為人知的　　　program〔'progræm〕*n.* 計劃
> wish〔wɪʃ〕*v.* 希望　　　trained〔trend〕*adj.* 受過訓練的
> staff〔stæf〕*n.* 工作人員　　　interview〔'ɪntɚˌvju〕*v.* 面談；審查
> potential〔pə'tɛnʃəl〕*adj.* 可能的　　　donor〔'donɚ〕*n.* 捐贈者

They screen out those whose blood may not be safe for transfusion, and then a pint of blood is taken from the donor's arm. <u>⁵(B) The donor may feel a little weak afterwards.</u> But a doughnut and a cup of coffee are enough to put him quickly on his feet again.

他們必須過濾掉一些人，因為那些人的血可能不安全，不適合用來輸血，然後再從捐血者的手臂上，抽取一品脫的血。事後，捐血者可能會覺得有點虛弱。但是只要一個甜甜圈和一杯咖啡，就足以使他們很快地復原。

> ***screen out*** （經篩選）去除
> pint〔paɪnt〕*n.* 品脫（容量單位）
> weak〔wik〕*adj.* 虛弱的　　　afterwards〔'æftɚwɚdz〕*adv.* 之後
> doughnut〔'donət〕*n.* 甜甜圈　　　***on one's feet*** 復原；康復

TEST 35

說明： 第 1 至 5 題，每題一個空格。請依文意在文章後所提供的 (A) 到 (E) 選項中分別選出最適當者。

A woman was asked by MSN, Microsoft's online service, to go to a website and re-enter her credit-card number. She thought it was strange and told her son. He felt suspicious, took the e-mail to his employer, Microsoft, and began a hunt to find a phisher.

____1____ A phisher sends out large numbers of messages in the form of e-mails, claiming to be from a bank or a company like Citicorp or MSN. The mail says there's something wrong with your account and asks you to link to a genuine-looking website so that you can fix it.

____2____ An estimated 100 million phishing e-mails go out every day, with losses of billions of dollars a year. Because these investigations are so complicated, law enforcement can be hesitant to take action. At the end of 2003, Microsoft took the initiative in pursuit of the case itself, filing suit against unknown John Does, so it could use court orders to find out who the false website was linked to. ____3____ Thus began, a long search focused on finding the owner of the false website.

Every website has an Internet address which can be traced to the service that hosts it, leading to other addresses, assigned by other ISPs. __4__ Round one was a company in San Diego. Round two was another hosting service in that area. Round three led to a free service in Europe, where Microsoft had no legal power to demand the identity of the address holder. __5__ This led to yet another Internet address, controlled by a company in the United States. A court order to the company led back to Microsoft itself: the address was assigned to an MSN user. Now Microsoft knew that the quest was far from over: it was a fresh start of an "epic" hunt! 【北模】

(A) The mail path reached a dead end at an Internet service provider (ISP) in India.

(B) Fortunately, the operator, Andreas Griesser, hates phishers, and gave the information voluntarily.

(C) But the site is a false one, and after you enter personal information, the phisher can use it to buy goods under your name.

(D) With each "round" a court order had to be served to the hosting ISP to discover who was paying for the service.

(E) Phishing is a cybercrime that has emerged recently.

TEST 35 詳解

A woman was asked by MSN, Microsoft's online service, to go to a website and re-enter her credit-card number. She thought it was strange and told her son.

MSN，也就是微軟公司的線上服務，要求一名女士上一個網站，並重新輸入她的信用卡卡號。她覺得很奇怪，所以就把這件事告訴她兒子。

Microsoft〔'maɪkrə,sɔft〕*n.* 微軟公司
re-enter〔ri'ɛntɚ〕*v.* 重新輸入
credit-card〔'krɛdɪt,kɑrd〕*adj.* 信用卡的

He felt suspicious, took the e-mail to his employer, Microsoft, and began a hunt to find a phisher.

她兒子覺得很可疑，於是就把這封電子郵件帶去給他的老闆看，也就是微軟公司，然後他們就展開追蹤，以找出這個網路釣客。

suspicious〔sə'spɪʃəs〕*adj.* 懷疑的；可疑的
employer〔ɪm'plɔɪɚ〕*n.* 老闆；雇主　　hunt〔hʌnt〕*n.* 追蹤；搜索
phisher〔'fɪʃɚ〕*n.* 網路騙子；網路釣客（唸法和 fisher 相同，指以假的電子郵件或網頁爲誘餌，騙取他人信用卡號或帳號的人，其常見的手法，是將郵件上的寄件人欄位改爲政府單位或知名大企業）

[1](E) Phishing is a cybercrime that has emerged recently. A phisher sends out large numbers of messages in the form of e-mails, claiming to be from a bank or a company like Citicorp or MSN.

網路釣魚是最近才出現的網路犯罪。網路釣客會以電子郵件的方式，大量寄出訊息，並聲稱該訊息是來自銀行或公司，像是花旗公司或 MSN。

phishing (ˈfɪʃɪŋ) *n.* 網路釣魚　*adj.* 網路釣魚的
cybercrime (ˈsaɪbəˈkraɪm) *n.* 網路犯罪
emerge (ɪˈmɝdʒ) *v.* 出現　　recently (ˈrisn̩tlɪ) *adv.* 最近
send out 寄出；送出　　***large numbers of*** 大量的
message (ˈmɛsɪdʒ) *n.* 訊息　　form (fɔrm) *n.* 形式
in the form of 以～形式　　claim (klem) *v.* 聲稱

The mail says there's something wrong with your account and asks you to link to a genuine-looking website so that you can fix it. [2](C) But the site is a false one, and after you enter personal information, the phisher can use it to buy goods under your name.
那封郵件寫著，你的帳戶有問題，並要求你連結到一個看來像是眞的的網站去處理。但是那個網站是假的，而且在你輸入個人資料之後，網路釣客就可以利用這些資料，以你的名義購買商品。

account (əˈkaʊnt) *n.* 帳戶　　link (lɪŋk) *v.* 連結 < *to* >
genuine (ˈdʒɛnjuɪn) *adj.* 眞的　　looking (ˈlʊkɪŋ) *adj.* 似乎是…的
fix (fɪks) *v.* 解決；處理　site (saɪt) *n.* 位置；地點 (在此指「網址」)
false (fɔls) *adj.* 假的　　personal (ˈpɝsn̩l̩) *adj.* 個人的
information (ˌɪnfəˈmeʃən) *n.* 資料　　goods (gʊdz) *n. pl.* 商品
under one's ***name*** 以某人的名義 (= *under the name of sb.*)

An estimated 100 million phishing e-mails go out every day, with losses of billions of dollars a year. Because these investigations are so complicated, law enforcement can be hesitant to take action.
據估計，每天都有一億封網路釣魚的電子郵件被寄出去，而這些郵件一年會造成好幾十億的損失。因爲調查太複雜，所以執法單位可能會猶豫要不要採取行動。

estimated (ˈɛstəˌmetɪd) *adj.* 估計的

loss (lɔs) *n.* 損失　　billion (ˈbɪljən) *n.* 十億

investigation (ɪnˌvɛstəˈgeʃən) *n.* 調查

complicated (ˈkɑmpləˌketɪd) *adj.* 複雜的

law enforcement　*n.* 執法；執法機構 (= *law enforcement agencies*)

hesitant (ˈhɛzətənt) *adj.* 猶豫的　　***take action*** 採取行動

At the end of 2003, Microsoft took the initiative in pursuit of the case itself, filing suit against unknown John Does, so it could use court orders to find out who the false website was linked to.

在二○○三年底時，微軟公司自己主動追蹤這件案子，並控告那些無名氏，這樣它們就可以利用法院命令，來找出假網站是連到誰那裡去。

initiative (ɪˈnɪʃɪˌetɪv) *n.* 主動　　***take the initiative*** 採取主動

pursuit (pɚˈsut) *n.* 追蹤　　***in pursuit of*** 追蹤

case (kes) *n.* 案件；事件　　file (faɪl) *v.* 提出 (訴訟等)

suit (sut) *n.* 訴訟　　***file suit against*** 控告

unknown (ʌnˈnon) *adj.* 不知名的　　***John Doe*** 【法律】約翰・多伊

　　【訴訟程序中對不知姓名的當事人假設的稱呼】；普通人；無名氏

court (kort) *n.* 法院　　***court order*** 法院命令

[3](A) The mail path reached a dead end at an Internet service provider (ISP) in India. Thus began, a long search focused on finding the owner of the false website.

那封郵件的路徑終點，是到達位於印度的網路服務提供者。於是，漫長的調查就此展開，而調查的焦點，就是要找出假網站的擁有者。

path (pæθ) *n.* 路徑　　***dead end*** 盡頭；死巷

India (ˈɪndɪə) *n.* 印度　　***focus on*** 把焦點對準

Every website has an Internet address which can be traced to the service that hosts it, leading to other addresses, assigned by other ISPs.

每個網站都有網址，從網址可以追蹤到負責提供這項服務的機構，然後再通往其他網路服務提供者所指定的網址。

address (ə'drɛs) *n.* 位址；地址
trace (tres) *v.* 追蹤　　host (host) *v.* 負責；主辦
lead to 通往　　assign (ə'saɪn) *v.* 指定

[4](D) With each "round" a court order had to be served to the hosting ISP to discover who was paying for the service. Round one was a company in San Diego. Round two was another hosting service in that area.

每次都必須把法院命令送到負責的網路服務提供者那邊，才能找出付費使用這項服務的人。第一次是一家位於聖地牙哥的公司。第二次是該區域的另一家主辦業者。

round (raʊnd) *n.* 一次；回合
serve (sɝv) *v.* 送達（傳票、令狀）
hosting ('hostɪŋ) *adj.* 主辦的；負責的
discover (dɪ'skʌvɚ) *v.* 發現；找到　　***pay for*** 支付～的費用
San Diego (,sændi'ego) *n.* 聖地牙哥　　area ('ɛrɪə) *n.* 區域

Round three led to a free service in Europe, where Microsoft had no legal power to demand the identity of the address holder. [5](B) Fortunately, the operator, Andreas Griesser, hates phishers, and gave the information voluntarily.

第三次則是通往歐洲一家免費提供服務的公司,可是微軟在那裡沒有
法律上的權力,來要求他們說出網址所有人的身分。很幸運的是,該
公司的經營者,安卓亞士‧格利瑟,很討厭網路釣客,所以自願提供
那些資料。

> demand (dɪ'mænd) v. 要求說出
> identity (aɪ'dɛntətɪ) n. 身分　　holder ('holdɚ) n. 所有人
> fortunately ('fɔrtʃənɪtlɪ) adv. 幸運地
> operator ('ɑpə,retɚ) n. 經營者
> voluntarily ('vɑlən,tɛrəlɪ) adv. 自願地

This led to yet another Internet address, controlled by a company
in the United States. A court order to the company led back to
Microsoft itself: the address was assigned to an MSN user.
這些資料又通往了另一個網址,而該網址是由美國的一家公司所控制。
但針對該公司所發出的法院命令,最後卻又回到微軟公司本身:因為那
個網址是由 MSN 的使用者所指定的。

> yet (jɛt) adv. 又

Now Microsoft knew that the quest was far from over: it was a
fresh start of an "epic" hunt!
微軟現在才知道,調查沒那麼快結束:這只是重新開始一場「大規模」
的搜索!

> quest (kwɛst) n. 追求;調查研究
> *far from over* 遠遠沒有結束
> fresh (frɛʃ) adj. 重新的
> epic ('ɛpɪk) adj. 極大規模的

TEST 36

說明： 第 1 至 5 題，每題一個空格。請依文意在文章後所提供的 (A) 到 (E) 選項中分別選出最適當者。

World War II gave us a sad example of a translation problem. By July 1945, Germany and Italy had already surrendered to the Allies. __1__ During the first weeks of July, Japan's premier thought over this demand. __2__ At the conference, he said that his country would *mokusatsu* the demand. But the use of the word *mokusatsu* was a very unfortunate choice. __3__ It can mean either "to consider" or "to take no notice of." The premier intended the first meaning, but the Allies understood the second. Thus the Allies believed that Japan had rejected their demand. __4__ This mistranslation made the U.S. decide to send B-29s with atomic bombs to the cities of Hiroshima and Nagasaki. __5__ 【北模】

(A) This word has two meanings.

(B) Finally, he called a press conference.

(C) But in fact the Japanese government was still considering it.

(D) Soon after this, the Allies demanded that Japan also surrender.

(E) If *mokusatsu* had been translated correctly, the atomic bombs might never have been dropped.

TEST 36 詳解

World War II gave us a sad example of a translation problem.
By July 1945, Germany and Italy had already surrendered to the
Allies.

第二次世界大戰就是個因為翻譯出問題，而釀成悲劇的例子。到了
一九四五年七月，德國和義大利已經向同盟國投降了。

> translation〔træns'leʃən〕*n.* 翻譯　　surrender〔sə'rɛndə〕*v.* 投降
> ally〔'ælaɪ〕*n.* 同盟　　***the Allies*** 同盟國

---

[1](D) Soon after this, the Allies demanded that Japan also surrender.
During the first weeks of July, Japan's premier thought over this
demand. [2](B) Finally, he called a press conference.

不久之後，同盟國要求日本也要投降。在七月的頭幾週，日本首相一直
在考慮這項要求。最後，他召開了記者會。

> ***soon after*** ~　~之後不久　　demand〔dɪ'mænd〕*v., n.* 要求
> premier〔'primɪə, prɪ'mɪr〕*n.* 首相　　***think over*** 考慮
> call〔kɔl〕*v.* 召開（會議）　　press〔prɛs〕*n.* 媒體；新聞界
> conference〔'kɑnfərəns〕*n.* 會議　　***press conference*** 記者招待會

At the conference, he said that his country would *mokusatsu* the
demand. But the use of the word *mokusatsu* was a very unfortunate
choice.

在記者會上，他說他的國家會 mokusatsu 這項要求。但是用 mokusatsu
這個字，是很不恰當的選擇。

> unfortunate〔ʌn'fɔrtʃənɪt〕*adj.* 不幸的；不恰當的
> choice〔tʃɔɪs〕*n.* 選擇

³(A) <u>This word has two meanings.</u> It can mean either "to consider" or "to take no notice of." The premier intended the first meaning, but the Allies understood the second.

這個字有兩個意思。它可以指「考慮」，或是「漠視」。首相指的是第一個意思，而同盟國卻以爲是第二個意思。

> meaning ('minɪŋ) *n.* 意思　　mean (min) *v.* 意思是
> consider (kən'sɪdɚ) *v.* 考慮　　notice ('notɪs) *n.* 注意
> ***take no notice of*** 不注意　　intend (ɪn'tɛnd) *v.* 意圖；意指
> understand (,ʌndɚ'stænd) *v.* 以爲；認爲

Thus the Allies believed that Japan had rejected their demand. ⁴(C) <u>But in fact the Japanese government was still considering it.</u>

於是同盟國認爲日本拒絕了他們的要求，但事實上，日本政府還在考慮。

> thus (ðʌs) *adv.* 因此；於是　　reject (rɪ'dʒɛkt) *v.* 拒絕

This mistranslation made the U.S. decide to send B-29s with atomic bombs to the cities of Hiroshima and Nagasaki. ⁵(E) <u>If *mokusatsu* had been translated correctly, the atomic bombs might never have been dropped.</u>

翻譯錯誤使美國決定派遣 B-29 轟炸機，帶著原子彈去轟炸廣島和長崎這兩個城市。如果 mokusatsu 有被正確地翻譯出來的話，那麼原子彈就絕不會被投擲下去。

> mistranslation (,mɪstræns'leʃən) *n.* 翻譯錯誤
> send (sɛnd) *v.* 派遣　　atomic (ə'tamɪk) *adj.* 原子的
> bomb (bam) *n.* 炸彈　　***atomic bomb*** 原子彈
> Hiroshima ('hɪrə'ʃimə) *n.* 廣島
> Nagasaki (,nægə'saki) *n.* 長崎　　drop (drap) *v.* 投下

TEST 37

Hundreds of different species of plants and animals have arrived in the United States. ___1___ Some of these new "residents" have caused problems for agriculture or for the environment. The Mediterranean fruit fly, for example, arrived in California on some imported fruit in the 1970s.

___2___ In California, however, it multiplied very quickly. Soon the California fruit industry was in trouble. The government had to take serious measures, including using lots of chemicals to try to kill the flies. However, they have not managed to get rid of the fly altogether.

___3___ It may not harm us directly, but it may change the environment. And that may cause problems for the plants or animals that were living there before. Loosestrife is a plant that came to America sometime in the 19th century. It may have been carried as seeds on the back of some sheep from Europe. Or someone may have brought the seeds to plant in their garden. ___4___ It is a pretty plant, with purple or pink flowers. But when a lot of loosestrife grows in one place, other plants cannot grow there. The birds and small animals that depend on those other plants cannot stay there, either. ___5___

【中山女中期中考】

(A) As loosestrife spreads, they may have trouble finding a place to live, and that may eventually lead to their extinction.

(B) In any case, loosestrife now grows along rivers and lakes all over North America.

(C) In its original home in the Mediterranean area, it had never caused much damage.

(D) Sometimes the damage caused by an immigrant species is not measurable in dollars.

(E) This number has increased greatly as international travel and business have increased.

TEST 37 詳解

Hundreds of different species of plants and animals have arrived in the United States. [1](E) <u>This number has increased greatly as international travel and business have increased.</u>

有數百種不同的動植物被運到美國去。而且隨著國際旅行和貿易的增加，這個數目也跟著大幅增加。

species〔'spiʃɪz〕*n. pl.* 種類　　plant〔plænt〕*n.* 植物
arrive〔ə'raɪv〕*v.* 到達；抵達
increase〔ɪn'kris〕*v.* 增加　　greatly〔'gretlɪ〕*adv.* 大大地
international〔͵ɪntə'næʃənḷ〕*adj.* 國際的
travel〔'trævḷ〕*n.* 旅行　　business〔'bɪznɪs〕*n.* 貿易

Some of these new "residents" have caused problems for agriculture or for the environment. The Mediterranean fruit fly, for example, arrived in California on some imported fruit in the 1970s.

在這些新「居民」當中，有些會對農業或環境造成問題。例如一九七〇年代時，某些進口水果將地中海果蠅帶到了加州。

resident〔'rɛzədənt〕*n.* 居民　　cause〔kɔz〕*v.* 導致；造成
agriculture〔'ægrɪ͵kʌltʃə〕*n.* 農業
environment〔ɪn'vaɪrənmənt〕*n.* 環境
Mediterranean〔͵mɛdətə'renɪən〕*adj.* 地中海的
fly〔flaɪ〕*n.* 蒼蠅　　***fruit fly*** 果蠅
California〔͵kælə'fɔrnjə〕*n.* 加州
imported〔ɪm'pɔrtɪd〕*adj.* 進口的

²(**C**) <u>In its original home in the Mediterranean area, it had never</u> <u>caused much damage.</u> In California, however, it multiplied very quickly. Soon the California fruit industry was in trouble.

在牠們原本的家鄉，也就是地中海地區，這些果蠅從來沒有造成多大的損害。但在加州，牠們繁殖得非常快。加州的水果業很快就陷入困境。

original〔ə'rɪdʒənḷ〕*adj.* 原本的
home〔hom〕*n.* 家鄉；生長地　　area〔'ɛrɪə〕*n.* 地區
damage〔'dæmɪdʒ〕*n.* 損失；損害
multiply〔'mʌltə͵plaɪ〕*v.* 繁殖
industry〔'ɪndəstrɪ〕*n.* 產業
trouble〔'trʌbḷ〕*n.* 困難；麻煩
be in trouble 陷入困境；有麻煩

The government had to take serious measures, including using lots of chemicals to try to kill the flies. However, they have not managed to get rid of the fly altogether.

政府必須採取一些重大措施，包括大量使用化學藥品來殺死這些果蠅。但是他們並沒有設法徹底消滅這些果蠅。

government〔'gʌvənmənt〕*n.* 政府　　take〔tek〕*v.* 採取
serious〔'sɪrɪəs〕*adj.* 重大的
measure〔'mɛʒɚ〕*n.* 措施
including〔ɪn'kludɪŋ〕*prep.* 包括
chemical〔'kɛmɪkḷ〕*n.* 化學藥品
manage〔'mænɪdʒ〕*v.* 設法　　***get rid of*** 擺脫；消滅
altogether〔͵ɔltə'gɛðɚ〕*adv.* 徹底地

³**(D)** Sometimes the damage caused by an immigrant species is not measurable in dollars. It may not harm us directly, but it may change the environment.

有時候，自國外引進的品種，會造成無法以金錢來衡量的損失。它可能沒有直接傷害我們，但卻會改變環境。

immigrant〔'ɪmə,grænt〕*adj.* 自國外引進的
measurable〔'mɛʒərəbḷ〕*adj.* 可測量的
harm〔harm〕*v.* 傷害　　directly〔də'rɛktlɪ〕*adv.* 直接地

And that may cause problems for the plants or animals that were living there before. Loosestrife is a plant that came to America sometime in the 19th century.

這樣一來，也會給之前就住在那裡的動植物帶來麻煩。珍珠菜這種植物，是在十九世紀的某個時候來到美國的。

Loosestrife〔'lus,straɪf〕*n.* 珍珠菜
sometime〔'sʌm,taɪm〕*adv.* 某時　　century〔'sɛntʃərɪ〕*n.* 世紀

It may have been carried as seeds on the back of some sheep from Europe. Or someone may have brought the seeds to plant in their garden.

可能是來自歐洲的綿羊在運入美國時，背上夾帶了珍珠菜的種子。也有可能是有人把種子帶回來，種在自己的庭園裡。

carry〔'kærɪ〕*v.* 攜帶；運送　　seed〔sid〕*n.* 種子
back〔bæk〕*n.* 背部　　sheep〔ʃip〕*n.* 綿羊
Europe〔'jurəp〕*n.* 歐洲　　plant〔plænt〕*v.* 種植
garden〔'gardṇ〕*n.* 庭園

[4](B) In any case, loosestrife now <u>grows along rivers and lakes all</u>
<u>over North America.</u> It is a pretty plant, with purple or pink
flowers. But when a lot of loosestrife grows in one place, other
plants cannot grow there.

不管是怎樣，目前在北美各地的河邊和湖邊，都長滿了珍珠菜。它是
一種美麗的植物，而且會開出紫色或粉紅色的花。但是當一個地方長
了大量的珍珠菜時，其他植物就無法在那裡生長。

> *in any case* 無論如何；不管怎樣　　grow〔gro〕*v.* 生長
> along〔əˈlɔŋ〕*prep.* 沿著
> *all over* 遍及　　North〔nɔrθ〕*adj.* 北部的
> pretty〔ˈprɪtɪ〕*adj.* 美麗的　　purple〔ˈpɜpl̩〕*adj.* 紫色的
> pink〔pɪŋk〕*adj.* 粉紅色的

The birds and small animals that depend on those other plants
cannot stay there, either. [5](A) <u>As loosestrife spreads, they may</u>
<u>have trouble finding a place to live, and that may eventually lead</u>
<u>to their extinction.</u>

而依賴那些植物的鳥類和小動物，也就無法待在那裡了。隨著珍珠菜
的散播，牠們可能很難找到住的地方，而且這麼一來，牠們最後可能
會滅絕。

> *depend on* 依賴　　*not…either* 也不…
> as〔əz〕*conj.* 隨著　　spread〔sprɛd〕*v.* 散播
> *have trouble + V-ing* 很難~
> eventually〔ɪˈvɛntʃʊəlɪ〕*adv.* 最後　　*lead to* 導致
> extinction〔ɪkˈstɪŋkʃən〕*n.* 滅絕；絕種

TEST 38

說明： 第 1 至 5 題，每題一個空格。請依文意在文章後所提供的 (A) 到 (E) 選項中分別選出最適當者。

Shy people don't enjoy being with others. ___1___ Some people feel shy occasionally, while others feel shy all the time. Some claim that shyness allows them to look at things more closely and to listen more completely.

___2___ Shy people feel uneasy in social situations. They are often too worried about what other people think of them to be relaxed. At work they dread having to speak at meetings or interact with their co-workers. Their feelings prevent them from making friends, trying new experiences, and achieving important goals in life.

___3___ Shyness is, to some extent, genetic. This means that some people, about 15 percent of us, are shy from birth. Even before being born, the hearts of shy children beat much faster than the hearts of other children. As newborns, these babies feel nervous and cry around others. As very young children, they seem afraid of new experiences. ___4___ Genetic traits can be changed. In fact, most of the children who are born shy lose their shyness over time. Positive experiences help the children to develop their feelings of self-esteem or self-worth.

＿＿5＿＿ A parent's praise for the child's accomplishments, as well as a tolerance for failure, is important. Unfortunately, however, not all children develop the confidence and experience to overcome their shyness. Some may suffer feelings of nervousness for many years. 【中山女中期末考】

(A) A shy child who is given the chance to develop an ability for music or sports will gain skills and the confidence to overcome shyness.

(B) Important research has shown some of the reasons for shyness.

(C) They feel very uncomfortable or embarrassed in any situation where others will notice or pay attention to them.

(D) But that does not mean that all shy babies necessarily become shy adults.

(E) But most people would agree that being shy puts people at a disadvantage.

TEST 38 詳解

Shy people don't enjoy being with others. [1](C) They feel very
uncomfortable or embarrassed in any situation where others will
notice or pay attention to them.

　　害羞的人不喜歡和別人在一起。在任何會被其他人注意到的情況，他
們都覺得很不自在或很尷尬。

　　　　uncomfortable〔ʌn'kʌmfɚtəbļ〕*adj.* 不自在的；困窘的
　　　　embarrassed〔ɪm'bærəst〕*adj.* 尷尬的　　notice〔'notɪs〕*v.* 注意到

Some people feel shy occasionally, while others feel shy all the
time. Some claim that shyness allows them to look at things more
closely and to listen more completely.

有些人是偶爾會害羞，而有些人卻是一直都很害羞。有些人宣稱，害羞
會讓他們看東西更仔細，而且聽到的事情更完整。

　　　　occasionally〔ə'keʒənḷɪ〕*adv.* 偶爾　　***all the time*** 一直；經常
　　　　claim〔klem〕*v.* 宣稱　　shyness〔'ʃaɪnɪs〕*n.* 害羞

[2](E) But most people would agree that being shy puts people at a
disadvantage. Shy people feel uneasy in social situations. They
are often too worried about what other people think of them to be
relaxed.

可是，大多數的人都一致認為，害羞會讓人處於不利的地位。在社交場
合中，害羞的人會覺得很不安。他們常常過度擔心別人對他們的看法，
以致於無法放輕鬆。

　　　　disadvantage〔,dɪsəd'væntɪdʒ〕*n.* 不利
　　　　put sb. at a disadvantage 置某人於不利的地位
　　　　uneasy〔ʌn'izɪ〕*adj.* 不安的

At work they dread having to speak at meetings or interact with their co-workers. Their feelings prevent them from making friends, trying new experiences, and achieving important goals in life.

在工作時，他們害怕必須在會議中發言，或是和同事互動。他們的感受使他們交不到朋友、不敢嘗試新的體驗，而且也無法達成重要的人生目標。

　　dread〔drɛd〕v. 害怕　　interact〔͵ɪntɚˋækt〕v. 互動

[3](B) Important research has shown some of the reasons for shyness. Shyness is, to some extent, genetic. This means that some people, about 15 percent of us, are shy from birth.

　　有個重要的研究說明了害羞的部分原因。在某種程度上，害羞是會遺傳的。意思就是說，在我們之中，大約有百分之十五的人，是天生就會害羞的。

　　extent〔ɪkˋstɛnt〕n. 程度　　*to some extent*　就某種程度而言
　　genetic〔dʒəˋnɛtɪk〕adj. 遺傳上的　　*from birth*　天生

Even before being born, the hearts of shy children beat much faster than the hearts of other children. As newborns, these babies feel nervous and cry around others.

害羞的孩子甚至是在出生之前，心臟就跳得比其他人要快很多。剛出生時，這些嬰兒就會緊張，所以會在別人身邊大哭。

　　beat〔bit〕v. (心臟) 跳動　　newborn〔ˋnjuˋbɔrn〕n. 新生兒

As very young children, they seem afraid of new experiences. [4](D) But that does not mean that all shy babies necessarily become shy adults. Genetic traits can be changed.

他們似乎從很小的時候，就會害怕新的體驗。但這並不表示所有害羞的嬰兒，長大後也一定都會害羞。遺傳的特性可能會改變。

　　necessarily〔ˋnɛsə͵sɛrəlɪ〕adv. 必定　　trait〔tret〕n. 特質；特性

In fact, most of the children who are born shy lose their shyness over time. Positive experiences help the children to develop their feelings of self-esteem or self-worth.

事實上，大多數天生就害羞的孩子，在一段時間過後，就不會再害羞了。
正面的經驗有助於培養孩子們的自尊。

> lose〔luz〕*v.* 解除；不再有　　***over time*** 經過一段時間
> positive〔'pɑzətɪv〕*adj.* 正面的
> self-esteem〔͵sɛlfə'stim〕*n.* 自尊
> self-worth〔'sɛlf'wɝθ〕*n.* 自尊（= *self-esteem*）

[5](A) A shy child who is given the chance to develop an ability for music or sports will gain skills and the confidence to overcome shyness. A parent's praise for the child's accomplishments, as well as a tolerance for failure, is important.

　　如果讓害羞的孩子有機會發展音樂或體育方面的才能，就可以增強他們克服害羞的能力和自信心。父母親要誇讚孩子的成就，以及容忍他們的失敗，這些都非常重要。

> overcome〔͵ovɚ'kʌm〕*v.* 克服　　praise〔prez〕*n.* 稱讚
> accomplishments〔ə'kɑmplɪʃmənts〕*n. pl.* 成就
> ***as well as*** 以及　　tolerance〔'tɑlərəns〕*n.* 容忍

Unfortunately, however, not all children develop the confidence and experience to overcome their shyness. Some may suffer feelings of nervousness for many years.

但遺憾的是，並非所有的孩子，都能培養出克服害羞的自信心和經驗。
有些人可能會被緊張的感覺困擾很多年。

> unfortunately〔ʌn'fɔrtʃənɪtlɪ〕*adv.* 遺憾地；不幸地
> suffer〔'sʌfɚ〕*v.* 遭受；經歷　　nervousness〔'nɝvəsnɪs〕*n.* 緊張

TEST 39

說明： 第 1 至 5 題，每題一個空格。請依文意在文章後所提供的 (A) 到 (E) 選項中分別選出最適當者。

A legend is a popular type of folk tale. ___1___ But myths describe events from antiquity and usually deal with religious subjects, such as the birth of a god. Legends tell of recognizable people and places and often take place in comparatively recent times. ___2___ Legends of superhuman accomplishments are often imaginary. ___3___ All societies have legends. ___4___ For example, John Henry was a legendary hero of black Americans, and Casey Jones of railroad workers. ___5___ They are no longer well known only to certain groups of people. 【北模】

(A) Over time, however, these figures have become national heroes.

(B) Some legends are based on real persons or events but many are entirely fictional.

(C) By contrast, legends about Washington and Lincoln are mostly exaggerations of their real qualities.

(D) In some ways, legends resemble myths, another type of folk tale.

(E) Most legends began as stories about heroes of a particular group of people.

TEST 39 詳解

A legend is a popular type of folk tale. **¹(D) In some ways, legends resemble myths, another type of folk tale.** But myths describe events from antiquity and usually deal with religious subjects, such as the birth of a god.

傳說是一種很受歡迎的民間故事。傳說在某些方面很像神話,而神話則是另一種民間故事。但是,神話都是描述古代的事,而且通常是有關宗教方面的主題,像是神的誕生。

legend ('lɛdʒənd) n. 傳說　　*folk tale* 民間故事
way (we) n. 方面　　resemble (rɪ'zɛmbl̩) v. 像
myth (mɪθ) n. 神話　　antiquity (æn'tɪkwətɪ) n. 古代;古代生活
deal with 討論;與～有關　　religious (rɪ'lɪdʒəs) adj. 宗教的
subject ('sʌbdʒɪkt) n. 主題;題材　　*such as* 像是

Legends tell of recognizable people and places and often take place in comparatively recent times. **²(B) Some legends are based on real persons or events but many are entirely fictional.**
傳說是敘述大家都認識的人物和地點,而且常是發生在近代。有些傳說是根據真實的人物或事件,但是,有許多是純屬虛構的。

tell of 談到
recognizable ('rɛkəg,naɪzəbl̩) adj. 可認識的;認得的
take place 發生　　comparatively (kəm'pærətɪvlɪ) adv. 相當地
recent ('risn̩t) adj. 最近的　　times (taɪmz) n. pl. 時代
be based on 根據　　entirely (ɪn'taɪrlɪ) adv. 完全地
fictional ('fɪkʃənl̩) adj. 虛構的

Legends of superhuman accomplishments are often imaginary.
³(C) By contrast, legends about Washington and Lincoln are mostly exaggerations of their real qualities.

與超乎常人的成就有關的傳說，經常都是虛構的。相較之下，華盛頓和林肯的傳說，則大多是誇大他們真正的特色。

> superhuman〔͵supəˈhjumən〕*adj.* 超乎常人的
> accomplishments〔əˈkɑmplɪʃmənts〕*n. pl.* 成就
> imaginary〔ɪˈmædʒə͵nɛrɪ〕*adj.* 虛構的　　　***by contrast*** 相較之下
> exaggeration〔ɪg͵zædʒəˈreʃən〕*n.* 誇張；誇大
> quality〔ˈkwɑlətɪ〕*n.* 特質；特色

All societies have legends.　**⁴(E) Most legends began as stories about heroes of a particular group of people.**　For example, John Henry was a legendary hero of black Americans, and Casey Jones of railroad workers.

每個社會都有傳說。大部份的傳說，都是始於某一群人的英雄故事。例如，約翰・亨利是美國黑人的傳奇英雄，而凱西・瓊斯則是鐵路工人的傳奇英雄。

> particular〔pəˈtɪkjələ〕*adj.* 特定的
> legendary〔ˈlɛdʒənd͵ɛrɪ〕*adj.* 傳說中的
> ***black American*** 美國黑人　　　railroad〔ˈrel͵rod〕*n.* 鐵路

⁵(A) Over time, however, these figures have become national heroes.
They are no longer well known only to certain groups of people.

然而，隨著時間的過去，這些人物都變成了國家英雄。他們的聲名大噪，認識他們的人不再僅限於某些群體。

> ***over time*** 隨著時間的過去　　　figure〔ˈfɪgjə〕*n.* 人物
> ***no longer*** 不再　　　***well known*** 有名的
> ***be well known to*** 被～所熟知　　　certain〔ˈsɜtn̩〕*adj.* 某些

TEST 40

說明： 第1至5題，每題一個空格。請依文意在文章後所提供的(A)到
(E) 選項中分別選出最適當者。

In the early 1800s, horses pulled wagons over
wooden rails. These were the first American trains.
These trains could go only a short distance. __1__

A big improvement was made in the 1830s.
The first steam engines were used. __2__ The
fire burned and turned the water inside the engine
into steam. The steam made pistons move back
and forth. The pistons moved rods that turned the
wheels. Wood was used for about the next forty
years.

After the Civil War, steam engines used coal
instead of wood. __3__ It was burned to heat
water and make steam in the same way that wood
was used.

From 1900 to 1935, the design of trains did not change much. Trains from these years are called the classic trains. Some people think these were the best trains ever made. ___4___ A classic train had a dining car, a lounge, and Pullman cars. The seats in a Pullman car turned into beds. Passengers could get a good night's sleep on their long trips.

Trains used the steam engine for about sixty years. In the 1930s the diesel engine appeared. The classic trains were replaced by streamliner trains. ___5___ 【台南女中期末考】

(A) Coal burned longer and made a better fuel.
(B) Today you might ride on a double-deck superliner train.
(C) They used wood as fuel to feed a fire.
(D) Many passengers rode on trains at this time.
(E) Only a few cars could be pulled at once.

TEST 40 詳解

In the early 1800s, horses pulled wagons over wooden rails. These were the first American trains. These trains could go only a short distance. ¹(E) Only a few cars could be pulled at once.

十九世紀初，由馬匹拉動的四輪馬車，是走在木製的軌道上。這些馬車就是美國最早的火車。但是這些火車只能走一小段距離。而且一次只能拉幾部車。

> wagon (ˈwægən) *n.* 四輪馬車
> wooden (ˈwʊdn̩) *adj.* 木製的　**at once** 同時

A big improvement was made in the 1830s. The first steam engines were used. ²(C) They used wood as fuel to feed a fire. The fire burned and turned the water inside the engine into steam. The steam made pistons move back and forth. The pistons moved rods that turned the wheels. Wood was used for about the next forty years.

在一八三〇年代，人們做了很大的改良。最早的蒸氣引擎開始啟用。人們在火裡添加木柴當燃料。火會加熱引擎裡的水，並使它變成水蒸氣。水蒸氣會讓活塞前後移動。活塞再使轉動車輪的活塞桿動起來。之後大約有四十年的時間，都是用木柴來當燃料。

> improvement (ɪmˈpruvmənt) *n.* 改良
> steam (stim) *adj.* 靠蒸氣推動的　*n.* 蒸氣
> engine (ˈɛndʒən) *n.* 引擎　fuel (ˈfjuəl) *n.* 燃料
> feed (fid) *v.* 添 (燃料)；助長　**turn A into B** 把 A 變成 B
> piston (ˈpɪstn̩) *n.* 活塞　**back and forth** 前後地
> rod (rɑd) *n.* 桿　wheel (hwil) *n.* 車輪

After the Civil War, steam engines used coal instead of wood. ³(A) Coal burned longer and made a better fuel. It was burned to heat water and make steam in the same way that wood was used.

南北戰爭之後，蒸氣引擎開始用煤來取代木柴。煤可以燃燒得比較久，所以是更好的燃料。人們用同樣的方式來燃燒煤，並使水在加熱之後產生水蒸氣。

Civil War （美國的）南北戰爭（發生於西元 1861-1865 年）
coal〔kol〕*n.* 煤　　***instead of*** 取代
make〔mek〕*v.* 成爲　　heat〔hit〕*v.* 加熱

From 1900 to 1935, the design of trains did not change much.
Trains from these years are called the classic trains. Some people think
these were the best trains ever made. [4](D) Many passengers rode on
trains at this time. 從一九〇〇年到一九三五年，火車的設計沒有太大的
改變。在這幾年間所製造的火車，被稱爲傳統火車。有些人認爲，這些火
車是有史以來最棒的火車。此時，很多旅客都是搭火車。

design〔dɪ'zaɪn〕*n.* 設計　　classic〔'klæsɪk〕*adj.* 經典的；傳統的
ever〔'ɛvɚ〕*adv.* 曾經；迄今　　passenger〔'pæsṇdʒɚ〕*n.* 旅客

A classic train had a dining car, a lounge, and Pullman cars. The seats
in a Pullman car turned into beds. Passengers could get a good night's
sleep on their long trips. 傳統火車上面有餐車、娛樂室和臥車。臥車裡的
座位被改成床。旅客可以在長途旅行中睡個好覺。

dine〔daɪn〕*v.* 用餐　　***dining car*** 餐車
lounge〔laʊndʒ〕*n.*（火車、輪船上的）娛樂室
Pullman〔'pʊlmən〕*n.* 臥車　　***Pullman car*** 臥車（= *Pullman*）

Trains used the steam engine for about sixty years. In the 1930s
the diesel engine appeared. The classic trains were replaced by
streamliner trains. [5](B) Today you might ride on a double-deck
superliner train. 大約有六十年的時間，火車都是使用蒸氣引擎。一九三
〇年代時，內燃機問世。傳統火車被流線型火車所取代。現在，你還可以
搭到雙層的超級火車。

diesel〔'disḷ〕*n.* 柴油機　　***diesel engine*** 內燃機
appear〔ə'pɪr〕*v.* 出現；問世　　replace〔rɪ'ples〕*v.* 取代
streamliner〔'strim,laɪnɚ〕*n.* 流線型火車　　deck〔dɛk〕*n.* 地板；層
double-deck〔'dʌbḷ'dɛk〕*adj.* 雙層的
superliner〔'supɚ,laɪnɚ〕*n.* 超級客車

TEST 41

說明： 第 1 至 5 題，每題一個空格。請依文意在文章後所提供的 (A) 到 (E) 選項中分別選出最適當者。

News is everywhere and serves many different functions. ___1___ News also provides facts and information. ___2___: a way to make money by selling advertising and newspapers and magazines. Sometimes news is propaganda or disinformation: a way to control a population. ___3___ We can't escape it. Every day we are bombarded by information from newspapers, magazines, television and the Internet.

"News" does not always mean something that is unquestionably true. Although the news seems to be based on facts, these facts are usually reported the way the media choose to report them. ___4___ Furthermore, many journalists and reporters sensationalize or dramatize a news event in order to make a story more interesting. ___5___ Therefore, as consumers of news we must learn to think critically about the news, the media, and the truth. 〔北模〕

(A) In addition, news is business

(B) But whatever news is, it is all around us.

(C) News gives instant coverage of important events.

(D) Unfortunately, sensationalism often prevents us from learning the truth and causes great pain to the people it exploits.

(E) For example, some information that appears as news is really only speculation or theories formed by the reporters.

TEST 41 詳解

News is everywhere and serves many different functions. [1](C) News gives instant coverage of important events. News also provides facts and information.

　　新聞無所不在，而且有許多不同的功能。新聞提供重要事件的即時報導。還有事實與資訊。

　　serve〔sɜv〕v. 符合；適合（目的、需要、用途）
　　function〔'fʌŋkʃən〕n. 功能　　　instant〔'ɪnstənt〕adj. 立即的
　　coverage〔'kʌvərɪdʒ〕n. 報導

[2](A) In addition, news is business: a way to make money by selling advertising and newspapers and magazines. Sometimes news is propaganda or disinformation: a way to control a population.

此外，新聞是一種事業：它藉由販賣廣告、報紙及雜誌來賺錢。有時候，新聞是一種宣傳，或是不實的報導：是種控制人們的方式。

　　in addition 此外　　　advertising〔'ædvə͵taɪzɪŋ〕n. 廣告
　　propaganda〔͵prɑpə'gændə〕n. 宣傳
　　disinformation〔͵dɪsɪnfə'meʃən〕n. 不正確的報導
　　population〔͵pɑpjə'leʃən〕n. 人口；人們

[3](B) But whatever news is, it is all around us. We can't escape it. Every day we are bombarded by information from newspapers, magazines, television and the Internet.

但是無論新聞是什麼，它總是充斥在我們身邊。我們無法避開它。我們每天被來自報紙、雜誌、電視，以及網際網路的資訊所轟炸。

　　escape〔ə'skep〕v. 避免；逃走　　　bombard〔bɑm'bɑrd〕v. 轟炸

"News" does not always mean something that is unquestionably true. Although the news seems to be based on facts, these facts are usually reported the way the media choose to report them.

「新聞」並不一定是百分之百眞實的。雖然新聞似乎是以事實爲根據,但媒體通常是以自己所選擇的方式,來報導這些事實。

> ***not always*** 不一定　　unquestionably〔ʌnˋkwɛstʃənəblɪ〕*adv.* 無疑地
> ***be based on*** 根據　　media〔ˋmidɪə〕*n.pl.* 媒體

⁴**(E)** For example, some information that appears as news is really only speculation or theories formed by the reporters. Furthermore, many journalists and reporters sensationalize or dramatize a news event in order to make a story more interesting.

舉例來說,有些看起來像新聞的資訊,實際上只是記者自己想出來的推測或理論。此外,許多新聞從業人員及記者,都會爲了讓報導更有趣,而譁衆取寵,或是將新聞事件戲劇化。

> appear〔əˋpɪr〕*v.* 似乎;看起來
> speculation〔͵spɛkjəˋleʃən〕*n.* 推測　　form〔fɔrm〕*v.* 想出
> journalist〔ˋdʒɝnḷɪst〕*n.* 新聞工作者;記者
> sensationalize〔sɛnˋseʃənḷ͵aɪz〕*v.* 使…聳人聽聞;譁衆取寵
> dramatize〔ˋdræmə͵taɪz〕*v.* 使戲劇化　　***in order to*** 爲了
> story〔ˋstorɪ〕*n.* 新聞報導

⁵**(D)** Unfortunately, sensationalism often prevents us from learning the truth and causes great pain to the people it exploits. Therefore, as consumers of news we must learn to think critically about the news, the media, and the truth.

遺憾的是,譁衆取寵往往使我們無法得知事實,而且還會對被報導出來的人,造成很大的痛苦。因此,身爲新聞的消費者,我們必須學習對新聞、媒體及事實的眞相,做批判性的思考。

> unfortunately〔ʌnˋfɔrtʃənɪtlɪ〕*adv.* 不幸地;遺憾地
> sensationalism〔sɛnˋseʃənḷ͵ɪzəm〕*n.* 聳人聽聞;煽情主義
> exploit〔ɪkˋsplɔɪt〕*v.* 報導　　consumer〔kənˋsumɚ〕*n.* 消費者
> critically〔ˋkrɪtɪkḷɪ〕*adv.* 批判性地

TEST 42

說明： 第 1 至 5 題，每題一個空格。請依文意在文章後所提供的 (A) 到 (E) 選項中分別選出最適當者。

Homebuyers can spend up to three months, and possibly more, looking for and purchasing a home. Their research begins with looking at housing ads, or driving through neighborhoods they are interested in. ___1___

Homebuyers should know how much they can afford. ___2___ So it's a good idea to look at your financial situation first. You might be surprised at how much you can borrow, especially when the interest rates are good. ___3___

You should never make an offer on a home without looking at other houses in the same neighborhood. Just as you would comparison-shop for a car or a computer, you should do a cost comparison on different homes for sale.

___4___ This information is available at local recorder's or assessor's offices, as well as through private companies or on the Internet. ___5___ For instance, maybe the seller needs to sell quickly and would accept a low offer. 【北模】

(A) You can do this by asking about recent sales of similar properties.

(B) It isn't worth your time to look for a new home if you can't really afford to buy one.

(C) Also, doing some research on the seller's motivation for selling will put you in a better position.

(D) Many first-time buyers will meet with a real estate agent to get help with finding and buying a home.

(E) Also, if you have some money saved for a down payment, your monthly payments may be lower than you think.

TEST 42 詳解

Homebuyers can spend up to three months, and possibly more, looking for and purchasing a home.

要買房子的人，可能會花長達三個月的時間來找房子和買房子，而且還有可能會花更久的時間。

up to 多達　　purchase ('pɜtʃəs) *v.* 購買

Their research begins with looking at housing ads, or driving through neighborhoods they are interested in. <u>[1](D) Many first-time buyers will meet with a real estate agent to get help with finding and buying a home.</u>

他們會從看房屋廣告開始搜尋，或是開車到他們有興趣的地區逛逛。很多第一次買房子的人，會和房屋仲介見面，要他們幫忙找房子和買房子。

> research (rɪ'sɜtʃ) *n.* 搜尋；調查　　ad (æd) *n.* 廣告
> through (θru) *prep.* 經過
> neighborhood ('nebə͵hʊd) *n.* 鄰近地區
> first-time ('fɜst'taɪm) *adj.* 初次的；首次的
> ***meet with*** 與…見面　　***real estate*** 不動產；房地產
> agent ('edʒənt) *n.* 經紀人

Homebuyers should know how much they can afford. <u>[2](B) It isn't worth your time to look for a new home if you can't really afford to buy one.</u> So it's a good idea to look at your financial situation first.

想買房子的人，應該要知道自己可以出得起多少錢。如果你其實買不起一間新房子，那就不值得花時間去找。所以先看看自己的財務狀況，是不錯的主意。

afford〔ə'ford〕v. 負擔得起　　worth〔wɜθ〕adj. 值得…的
financial〔fə'nænʃəl〕adj. 財務的
situation〔ˌsɪtʃu'eʃən〕n. 狀況

You might be surprised at how much you can borrow, especially
when the interest rates are good.　[3](E) Also, if you have some
money saved for a down payment, your monthly payments may be
lower than you think.
你可能會對自己可以借到多少錢感到驚訝,尤其是當利率很低時。還有,
如果你有存錢要付頭期款,那麼你每個月要繳的錢,會比你想像的低。

borrow〔'baro〕v. 借(入)　　especially〔ə'spɛʃəlɪ〕adv. 尤其是
interest rates 利率　　good〔gud〕adj. 適宜的;有利的
save〔sev〕v. 存(錢)　　down〔daun〕adj. 頭款的
a down payment 頭期款　　monthly〔'mʌnθlɪ〕adj. 每月的
payment〔'pemənt〕n. 支付;金額

You should never make an offer on a home without looking at
other houses in the same neighborhood.　Just as you would
comparison-shop for a car or a computer, you should do a cost
comparison on different homes for sale.
　在還沒有看過同一個地區的其他房子之前,你絕不應該出價買房子。
就像你會貨比三家後,再買車子或電腦,所以你也應該比較一下不同房
子的售價。

make an offer 提議;提供;出價
comparison〔kəm'pærəsn̩〕n. 比較
comparison-shop〔kəm'pærəsn̩ˌʃap〕v. 邊比較邊採購 < *for* >
cost〔kɔst〕n. 價格　　*for sale* 出售的

[4](A) <u>You can do this by asking about recent sales of similar</u> <u>properties.</u> This information is available at local recorder's or assessor's offices, as well as through private companies or on the Internet.

你可以詢問一下最近出售的類似房地產，好做個比較。這些資訊可以在當地地方法院的推事辦公室，或是稅額審查員的辦公室取得，也可以透過私人公司或在網路上找到。

recent ('risṇt) *adj.* 最近的　　similar ('sɪmələ) *adj.* 類似的
property ('prɑpətɪ) *n.* 房地產
available (ə'veləbḷ) *adj.* 可獲得的　　local ('lokḷ) *adj.* 當地的
recorder (rɪ'kɔrdə) *n.* 書記員；地方法院推事
assessor (ə'sɛsə) *n.* 稅額審查員　　***as well as*** 以及
through (θru) *prep.* 透過
private ('praɪvɪt) *adj.* 私人的

[5](C) <u>Also, doing some research on the seller's motivation for selling</u> <u>will put you in a better position.</u> For instance, maybe the seller needs to sell quickly and would accept a low offer.

另外，調查一下賣方出售房子的動機，會使你處於比較有利的地位。例如，也許賣方需要很快把房子賣掉，所以會接受較低的出價。

also ('ɔlso) *adv.* 此外
research (rɪ'sɝtʃ , 'risɝtʃ) *n.* 研究；調查
motivation (ˌmotə'veʃən) *n.* 動機
position (pə'zɪʃən) *n.* 地位
for instance 例如　　accept (ək'sɛpt) *v.* 接受
offer ('ɔfə) *n.* 出價

劉毅英文家教班成績優異同學獎學金排行榜

姓名	學校	總金額	姓名	學校	總金額	姓名	學校	總金額
賴宣佑	成淵高中	148050	張宛茹	基隆女中	17000	陳聖妮	中山女中	11100
王千	中和高中	91400	林政瑋	板橋高中	16600	呂濬瑺	成功高中	11100
翁一銘	中正高中	79350	郭權	建國中學	16600	劉苳琳	板橋高中	11100
呂芝瑩	內湖高中	52850	林學典	格致高中	16500	陳瑾瑜	中平國中	11000
吳宥龠	縣中山國中	50300	張雅婷	海山高中	16250	蔡岳峰	長安國中	11000
楊玄詳	建國中學	41400	蔡欣儒	百齡高中	16200	應奇穎	建國中學	10900
謝家綺	板橋高中	39000	洪子晴	大同高中	16100	賴品臻	明倫高中	10700
趙啓鈞	松山高中	34450	林怡廷	景美女中	15900	謝承孝	大同高中	10600
丁哲沛	成功高中	34250	秦嘉欣	華僑高中	15800	柯博軒	成功高中	10500
陳學蒨	再興高中	34100	潘羽薇	丹鳳高中	15600	黃浩銓	建國中學	10500
王芊蓁	北一女中	33650	邱瀞葶	縣格致中學	15600	司徒皓平	建國中學	10300
袁妤蓁	武陵高中	32750	劉裕心	中和高中	15550	吳思慧	景美女中	10300
吳書軒	成功高中	30600	施衍辰	成功高中	15500	呂家榮	陽明高中	10150
蔡佳容	北一女中	30450	李品萱	松山家商	15500	陳貞穎	中山女中	10000
蔡佳恩	建國中學	28500	陳品文	建國中學	15000	李之琳	永春國小	10000
許晏魁	竹林高中	28350	蘇柏中	師大附中	15000	李欣蓉	格致高中	10000
徐柏庭	延平高中	28200	許弘儒	成功高中	14700	孔爲亮	龍山國中	10000
呂佾蓁	南湖高中	27850	李怡芗	和平高中	14600	李宸馨	北一女中	9700
何宇屏	輔仁大學	27400	周欣穎	圖三重高中	14400	陳怡靜	北一女中	9700
王挺之	建國中學	27100	劉詩玟	北一女中	14300	廖彥綸	師大附中	9700
林祐瑋	耕莘護專	27050	楊姿芳	成淵高中	14100	羅映婷	內壢高中	9600
黃棨覬	北一女中	26550	劉秀慧	進修生	14100	陳亭如	北一女中	9600
張祐寧	建國中學	26000	林姿妤	丹鳳高中	13900	黃盟凱	圖三重高中	9600
黃靖淳	師大附中	25450	林書沛	薇閣高中	13900	林瑞軒	基隆高中	9600
蕭允惟	景美女中	25300	劉若盈	松山家商	13600	王簡群	華江高中	9550
黃筱雅	北一女中	25000	王雯琦	政大附中	13600	簡士益	格致高中	9500
趙祥安	新店高中	24600	方冠予	北一女中	13500	鄭涴心	板橋高中	9400
許嘉容	北市商	24400	曹傑	松山高中	13250	廖瓨軒	武陵高中	9400
羅之勵	大直高中	23800	陳瑾慧	北一女中	13200	劉良逸	台中一中	9300
練冠霆	板橋高中	23400	林政穎	中崙高中	13100	黃建發	永平高中	9300
王廷鎧	建國中學	23300	黃小榕	中崙高中	13000	黃靖燐	建國中學	9300
楊于萱	新莊高中	23200	洪采媚	北一女中	12900	劉哲銘	建國中學	9250
盧安	成淵高中	22300	蔡瑄庭	南湖高中	12500	陳冠儒	大同高中	9200
李佳珈	新莊高中	22300	粘書耀	師大附中	12500	蘇倍陞	板橋高中	9200
董澤元	再興高中	21800	劉婷婷	板橋高中	12400	吳柏諭	裕民國小	9150
許瑋峻	延平高中	21700	宋才聞	成功高中	12300	林怡瑄	大同高中	9100
陳婕峰	大理高中	21100	張馥雅	北一女中	12100	阮鎂儒	北一女中	9100
王裕堂	成淵高中	21100	邱馨荷	市中山國中	12000	徐浩倫	成功高中	9100
張祐銘	延平高中	20950	吳凱恩	復旦高中	12000	劉禹廷	板橋高中	9100
蔡欣伶	新店高中	20500	鄭晴	北一女中	11700	徐健智	松山高中	9100
陳冠揚	南湖高中	20400	陳昕	麗山高中	11700	邱雅蘋	聖心女中	9100
林悅婷	北一女中	19400	蔡承紜	復興高中	11650	曹家榕	大同高中	9000
吳灃晉	中正高中	18900	范詠琪	中山女中	11600	藍珮瑜	北一女中	9000
蘇芳萱	北一女中	18500	何俊毅	師大附中	11600	胡家瑜	桃園國中	9000
郭學豪	和平高中	18500	盧昱瑋	格致高中	11550	陳宣蓉	中山女中	8800
許瓊方	北一女中	18300	陳書毅	成功高中	11400	潘育誠	成功高中	8800
林侑緯	建國中學	17800	林份	林口高中	11400	黃新雅	松山高中	8600
林述君	松山高中	17550	劉俐妤	中山女中	11300	何宜臻	板橋高中	8500
郭子瑄	新店高中	17200	黃鈺雯	永春高中	11200	蔣詩媛	華僑高中	8400
陳柏諺	師大附中	17000	劉仁誠	建國中學	11200	劉妍君	新店高中	8400

劉毅英文教育機構

台北本部：台北市許昌街17號6F（捷運M8出口斜面・學藝補習班）　TEL：（02）2389-5212
台中總部：台中市三民路三段125號7F（光南文具批發樓上・劉毅補習班）　TEL：（04）2221-8861
www.learnschool.com.tw

指考篇章結構

主　　　編／劉　毅

發　行　所／學習出版有限公司　　　　☎ (02) 2704-5525

郵　撥　帳　號／05127272 學習出版社帳戶

登　記　證／局版台業 2179 號

印　刷　所／裕強彩色印刷有限公司

台 北 門 市／台北市許昌街 10 號 2 F　　☎ (02) 2331-4060

台灣總經銷／紅螞蟻圖書有限公司　　☎ (02) 2795-3656

美國總經銷／Evergreen Book Store　　☎ (818) 2813622

本公司網址　www.learnbook.com.tw

電 子 郵 件　learnbook@learnbook.com.tw

售價：新台幣二百二十元正

2014 年 9 月 1 日新修訂

ISBN 978-957-519-876-3